Penguin Books C 2378
The Mouse

Georges Simenon was born at Liège in Belgium in 1903.
At sixteen he began work as a journalist on the *Gazette de Liège*.
He has published over one hundred and eighty novels in
his own name, sixty-seven of which belong to the Inspector
Maigret series, and his work has been published in
thirty-two languages. He has had a great influence upon
French cinema, and more than forty of his novels have
been filmed.

Simenon's novels are largely psychological. He describes
hidden fears, tensions, and alliances beneath the surface of
bourgeois family life, which suddenly explode into violence
and crime. André Gide wrote to him: 'You are living on a
false reputation – just like Baudelaire or Chopin. But nothing
is more difficult than making the public go back on a too
hasty first impression. You are still the slave of your first
successes and the reader's idleness would like to put a stop
to your triumphs there. . . . You are much more *important*
than is commonly supposed'; and François Mauriac wrote:
'I am afraid I may not have the courage to descend right to
the depths of this nightmare which Simenon describes with
such unendurable art.'

Simenon has travelled a great deal and once lived on a cutter,
making long journeys of exploration round the coasts of
northern Europe. He is married and has four children, and
lives near Lausanne in Switzerland. He enjoys riding,
fishing, and golf.

Georges Simenon

The Mouse

Translated from the French by
Robert Baldick

Penguin Books

Penguin Books Ltd, Harmondsworth, Middlesex, England
Penguin Books Inc., 3300 Clipper Mill Road, Baltimore 11, Md, U.S.A.
Penguin Books Pty Ltd, Ringwood, Victoria, Australia

M. La Souris first published in France 1938
This translation published in Penguin Books 1966
This translation copyright © Penguin Books Ltd, 1966

Made and printed in Great Britain by
Cox & Wyman Ltd, London, Reading and Fakenham
Set in Monotype Garamond

Chapter One
The Silences of
Inspector Grumpy

It was just after 11.12 when the door of the police station opened. The two police motor-cyclists who were playing draughts raised their heads. The sergeant, who was smoking his pipe behind the black wooden desk, also straightened up, but, even before seeing the new arrival, he knew who it was, for a familiar voice said:

'I tell you, don't push me around, young man! You don't know who you're dealing with . . . Well, well, if it isn't *my* sergeant who's on duty!'

The day duty was nearing its end. In just over forty minutes the night shift would be taking over the station. The sergeant, who was a fat man, had unbuttoned his tunic, and Inspector Lognon, in plain clothes, was gloomily following the motor-cyclists' game.

It had been raining since eight o'clock that evening, one of those downpours which seem to soak you more than the rest, and which often occur all of a sudden at the end of a warm spring day. There was a gala performance at the Opera. You could tell that by the number of cars and, above all, the number of liveried chauffeurs you could hear chatting on the pavement.

On the other hand, none of the policemen from the local station, even those on duty inside the Opera itself, knew what was being performed.

What mattered was that it had been raining, that it was still raining, that the policemen would come back with their capes dripping, and that, as always happens when the road way is slippery, there had been three road accidents on the Boulevard des Italiens alone.

There were fewer hawkers of course, in fact, just one flower-seller who had just been brought in, and who was sitting beside her basket, knitting a child's sock in blue wool.

Altogether an ordinary evening. The sergeant was unhurriedly entering the accidents in the bulky black book which he would be handing over before long to his colleague on night duty.

The old man had arrived just at the right moment.

'Will you tell him, Sergeant, that the old Mouse mustn't be pushed around like that . . .'

The policeman who had brought him in still did not relax his grip. He was holding him by the shoulder or, rather, he had taken hold of the shoulder of the jacket and seemed to be lifting the little old man into the air like a puppet. He was a young fair-haired, pink-cheeked policeman, all fresh and new. The sergeant growled:

'Let go of him, Bonvoisin!'

And as there was a hint of sternness in his voice, the Mouse said triumphantly:

'You heard that? What have I been telling you all the way from the Madeleine?'

He tugged at his limp jacket, caught sight of Inspector Lognon, and gave him a wink.

When the old Mouse did not spend the night at the Opera police station, it was because he had been given a bed at the Champs-Élysées station, installed in the basement of the Grand Palais. Bonvoisin was new to the district, otherwise he would not have bothered to take his notebook out of his pocket, as if to make a regular report.

'You can go,' the sergeant said to him, relighting his pipe.

'Just a minute,' the Mouse broke in. 'If you don't mind, I need this young man's evidence.'

The old man was short and thin, with extraordinarily mobile and mischievous eyes, red hair turning a dirty white, and a very personal manner of wearing old clothes which were too big for him with an almost elegant aplomb.

'I'd be glad if you would listen too, Inspector . . . After all, it isn't often that something sensational happens to me . . .'

A little earlier, when they had seen the Mouse come in, they had known already that they were in for a comic act. It was a tradition, especially when the sergeant had enough time.

'You mean that at long last I've got you for vagrancy?' asked the station chief.

For that to happen, the Mouse would have had to have neither home, nor money. Now for months and months, for years in fact, while he had never had a fixed address, it had been impossible to catch him without a few coppers in his pocket. Sometimes he was searched. Nothing was found. But just as they were beginning to triumph, he would suddenly give a queer smile and take a five-franc piece out of some fold of his rags.

'Sergeant, I'd like you to put down in your report that your policeman arrested me on the terrace of a café at the Madeleine just as I was asking Léa for four francs . . .'

And he turned towards the plain-clothes Inspector Lognon, who was chiefly concerned with the prostitutes in the licensed brothels and the brasseries. Lognon, to have done with it, nodded his agreement, because naturally he knew Léa.

'Why four francs?' asked the sergeant in surprise.

'Because I wanted to take a taxi to come here, and with the tip that costs about four francs.'

It was at about this moment that Lognon stopped taking

this conversation lightly. Perhaps he noticed something disturbing in the Mouse's voice? True, the old man was in the habit of putting on his little act, and he was only happy when the audience rocked with laughter. But this time, wasn't there a gleam of anxiety in his eyes?

Lognon said nothing. He was not the man to waste his words. He stayed in his corner, as solemn and grumpy as usual.

The sergeant, for his part, carried on the conversation with the mock seriousness of a ringmaster questioning a clown in a circus.

'Why, were you afraid of getting wet?'

'No. But I was afraid of pickpockets.'

The Mouse had obtained the effect he wanted. His eyes sparkled with laughter. He exulted at the sight of the two motor-cyclists interrupting their game to listen to him. With an innocent expression he confided to them:

'When you're not used to walking about with a fortune in your pocket ...'

Lognon was the only one who didn't smile. He had a bony face, with heavy features, jet-black hair, and eyebrows like thick black bars. With his stubborn gaze, he seemed to be always in pursuit of the solution of some difficult problem.

'Show it to us, this fortune of yours ... Ten francs? Fifteen francs? ... I warn you that if you've got fifteen francs to pay for a bed, I'm not going to put you up ...'

' Just a minute ... Get ready to write me out a receipt ...'

And the Mouse finally took out of his pocket a long yellow envelope like those which are used for sending business papers, and which are closed with a metal clip.

'Take this down,' he said with calculated solemnity. 'Afterwards you can draw up an inventory ... On Wednesday the twenty-third of June, at half past ten in the evening, in the Rue Royale, in front of the restaurant Maxim's Ugo

Mosselbach, alias the Mouse, aged sixty-eight, born at Bischwiller-sur-Moder in the Bas-Rhin, found in the public highway a yellow envelope containing . . .'

For a moment the sergeant had been taken aback. Then automatically, he had opened the envelope and glanced inside, and straight away he had started writing in spite of himself at the Mouse's dictation.

'Bischwiller with two *l*'s?'

'Yes, two *l*'s. Moder with only one *d* . . . As I was saying, an envelope containing . . .'

Inspector Lognon got up and, with his hands in his pockets, came and planted himself behind the sergeant. The two motor-cyclists came up too to have a look.

'I wonder if this isn't really a matter for the chief-inspector,' the tramp said all of a sudden. He was joking as usual. But what he was saying might be serious, and the sergeant hesitated, turning towards Lognon who shrugged his shoulders.

'Open it, anyway . . . seeing that you're drawing up an inventory . . .'

'. . . nine five-hundred-dollar bills pinned together, in other words four thousand five hundred dollars . . .'

There was a short silence. The sergeant had let his pipe go out again.

'How much is that in francs?' he asked in spite of himself.

'About sixty-five thousand francs,' the Mouse informed him. 'There's some more . . .'

Sure enough, the envelope contained a second wad, which they counted twice over because it consisted of forty-nine hundred-dollar bills. Why forty-nine and not fifty?

Finally, at the bottom, there remained two thousand-franc notes, and two of a hundred francs.

While the sergeant was writing, Lognon examined the old man with a gaze heavy with displeasure.

'You really found that in the street? And whereabouts in the street?'

'A few yards from Maxim's.'

'On the pavement?'

The yellow envelope was wet, but not as wet as it would have been if it had spent even as little as ten minutes in the gutter.

'Yes, on the pavement. Monsieur Jean saw me pick up the envelope . . . He wanted to see what was inside with me, but a car drew up with some customers . . .'

Lognon made a note of these details: Léa on the terrace of the café, the commissionaire at Maxim's.

'What do I do?' the sergeant asked in perplexity, turning towards the inspector.

It was the Mouse who replied.

'You give me a receipt. If after a year and a day nobody has claimed the envelope, the money will belong to me and I shall buy the old presbytery of Bischwiller-sur-Moder . . .'

Pirouetting like an actor taking a curtain call, he made as if to head for the door, but he must have known that he would not be allowed to leave, for he did a rapid about-turn as soon as he heard Lognon's voice.

'Just a minute!' the latter growled.

'An hour if you like, Inspector. You know that your wish is my command . . .'

'Come here.'

And without any warning he searched his pockets, felt his clothes.

'Take your shoes off.'

The Mouse went on playing the fool, wriggling his toes, for he had no socks on, and starting to take off his trousers, with an apology to the flower-seller.

'It's these gentlemen, you understand. Me, I'm all for decency, but . . .'

'That's enough!' said Lognon. 'Off you go to bed.'

'Can't I go and have a drink first? You must admit that it's rather hard on a fellow who's just been in possession of a hundred and fifty thousand francs . . .'

Lognon pushed him in front of him through a doorway. There, there were three cages, one for women, another for men, and the third for tramps who had not committed any offence. In this last cage, an old man was lying face-down on a plank bed and he did not move even when the gate was opened. On the other side, in the half-light a young woman was sitting as if she were in a waiting-room, with her hand-bag on her knee.

'Good night all the same,' sighed the Mouse. 'With all respect, you're worse than the sergeant . . .'

When, at eight o'clock in the morning, a policeman opened the gate, the Mouse got up like an old hand, picked up his greenish bowler hat, and, before going into the station, looked around for Lognon.

Theoretically, the inspector, who had been on night duty, ought not to have been there. But he was there, and the Mouse knew it. The old man even treated himself to the malicious pleasure of asking:

'Well, what did she say?'

He was referring to Léa and the other did not reply.

'I say, Inspector, it can't have been so easy with Maxim's, because that pavement belongs to the Eighth Arrondissement, so that it's no business of yours . . .'

Lognon looked at him without batting an eyelid, and lit a cigarette. The policeman pushed the Mouse towards the door, which, as it opened, flooded the station with sunlight. It was a splendid morning, with sunshine brighter than ever after the wet night. The metal shutters of a few shops could be heard creaking, and a smell of croissants was coming from the bars.

'I'll bet he's behind me,' thought the Mouse as he ambled

along the boulevards in the direction of the Faubourg Montmartre.

He was careful not to hurry and, above all, not to stop at any of the newspaper kiosks. He limped along, bending down now and then to pick up a cigarette end which he slipped into his pocket, and, without seeing him, he was aware of Lognon all the time on his heels.

Anyone would have thought that he did not know where he was going. At the Montmartre crossroads he hesitated, and took a few steps along the Faubourg Montmartre before finally going back along the Boulevard Poissonnière and stopping, three-quarters of an hour after leaving the police station, in front of the window of the offices of a morning paper.

Whew! So much the worse for Lognon, who must have followed his casual stroll. Now, in the most natural way in the world, the Mouse planted himself in front of the brass frames which each contained one page of the morning edition. He was not the only one to do this, for his neighbours, like himself, were treating themselves to a free perusal of the paper.

Page One: nothing! . . . Page Two: Nothing! . . . Page Three: a burglary, some shots fired in a bar in Montrouge . . .

A pane of glass protected the paper and in this pane the Mouse saw the reflection of Lognon who had planted himself behind him, right up against him, gloomy and patient. There were two of them in the Ninth Arrondissement squad, a fat inspector of forty-five, who was always good-humoured and was known as Inspector Smiler; and Lognon, who had been nicknamed Inspector Grumpy.

Page Four . . .

The Mouse was baffled, looked straight away at the Stop Press column, then, unconvinced, went back to Page One.

Lognon gave a start when the tramp swung round and asked him point-blank:

'Are you going to treat me to a coffee? Seeing that we're going the same way ...'

Then the inspector shrugged his shoulders, dug his hands into his pockets, and went off to the bus stop. This time he was not pretending. He went off home to the Place Constantin-Pecqueur, in the Eighteenth Arrondissement.

Meanwhile the Mouse sat down on a bench opposite the Théâtre du Gymnase.

What was worrying was the paper's silence. For as far as the rest was concerned the Mouse was fairly sure that he had not made the slightest mistake. Lognon could investigate as much as he liked. For Lognon was investigating and would go on investigating. But that was something the old man had brought upon himself, not so much out of a desire to show off as from a liking for play-acting.

He had a timetable all ready to serve up to the inspector. First of all, since Wednesday was his day for having soup at the Salvation Army kitchen, he had gone on board the barge moored at the Tuileries port at six o'clock, and the ladies in the capes could testify that he had left only about seven o'clock.

Ambling up the Champs-Élysées as far as the Ambassadeurs had taken him almost up to eight o'clock. People were already queueing at the theatre box office, and the Mouse had opened car doors until twenty past nine, for the audience at the Ambassadeurs has a habit of arriving late. There are theatres like that, and others where everybody is in his seat by half past eight, like the Porte-Saint-Martin.

In any case, the ticket-seller had seen him ...

The rest was a rather more far-fetched, but even so he would spin his little tale, that he had sheltered in the Rond-Point Métro station for an hour, and that then, with the intention of 'working' the crowd coming out of the Opera, he had gone down to the Place de la Concorde where he had turned up the Rue Royale. There, in front of Maxim's ...

That hung together, didn't it? Besides, a good alibi mustn't be too precise. Wasn't it because of the evidence of Jean of Maxim's and Léa that Lognon had started taking an interest in the affair?

Only the fact that there shouldn't be even a couple of lines in the paper! ... Was it possible that ...?

The Mouse got up. He had one franc forty left and he treated himself to a glass of white wine in a bar, before setting off for the Champs-Élysées.

Naturally the Métro and all the rest was a pack of lies. But the truth was even more fantastic.

Until twenty past nine, nothing unusual had happened: he had opened car doors. Only, as it was raining, he had collected only five francs, for people waited for the commissionaire who had the advantage of a huge red umbrella.

The Mouse had accordingly made for the cars parked along the Avenue Gabriel, for a chauffeur sometimes bought him a beer in return for looking after his car during the show.

Again, on account of the rain, which had started coming down hard, the chauffeurs stayed inside their cars, reading their papers.

There weren't many cars either. By the Rue de l'Élysée it was already finished, and the Mouse went on limping along aimlessly, going up to a big car a good hundred yards from the others.

Nothing could be lonelier at night than this part of Paris, with the dark gates of the Élysée and, into the bargain, the heavy drops falling from the leaves of the chestnut trees.

There was a man in the car, but he was not a chauffeur. He was in evening dress. The astonishing thing was that now the Mouse could no longer remember whether he had a black tie or a white tie, in other words whether he was wearing a dinner jacket or tails.

It was impossible to remember what he had on his head either. A soft hat? A crush-hat? Perhaps nothing at all? In any case, the old tramp retained the impression of a man with fair hair, very fair hair.

Things had happened so fast! The Mouse had opened the car door. His line was all ready, a line which marked him out from the ordinary run-of-the-mill beggars, for he never tried to arouse pity. Far from it! He wrinkled up his eyes and said in a humorous voice:

'Give me a couple of francs to go and have a beer, Your Highness.'

This time he hadn't had time to get to the end. He had scarcely opened the door before the man, who seemed to be sitting up straight, fell sideways with it. The Mouse had pushed him back with both hands; he had felt something slimy, and at the same time he had noticed a dark stain on the man's shirt front.

'None of that!' he had growled automatically. 'You can't do that to me . . .'

He was in a hurry to get away. To do that he had to shut the door again, otherwise the body would have rolled on to the pavement. He therefore pushed it back inside the car. He felt something fall on his foot.

'None of that! . . . None of that,' he kept saying.

Whew! The door was finally shut and the man must have collapsed on the seat. As for the old tramp, he picked up the object that had fallen on his foot, a thick wallet, and, after a glance around him, slipped it into his pocket.

He had not opened it straight away. He had even gone quite a way along the other side of the Champs-Élysées towards the Cours la Reine, where he had stopped under a gas lamp.

He had found a wad of ten five-hundred-dollar bills,

then fifty hundred-dollar bills, then the French notes plus one.

The fellow was dead, that was certain. The Mouse could have sworn that the body was already cold. Before opening the wallet, he had had to wipe his hands on the wet grass, and he had an unpleasant feeling that his skin was still sticky.

The fact remained that he had no time to lose. You don't get an opportunity like that twice in a lifetime, and if he wasn't to miss this one, he had to leave nothing to chance.

Above all, he had to act quickly. In one pocket of the wallet, the Mouse noticed a little photograph of a girl, a very crude photograph, like those they do for passports. There were also three red tickets, possibly cinema tickets. Finally an empty envelope which he left where it was.

'There's no hurry about all that,' he muttered.

However, on the envelope he read the name:

'Sir Archibald Landsburry.'

Then something which must have been an address in London. But he would see about that later.

First of all, he removed from the wads of notes one five-hundred-dollar bill, one hundred-dollar bill and one French banknote, which he left in the wallet. He got rid of the wallet as quickly as he could in the first flower-bed he came to, a bed of tulips, slipping the thing under a few inches of earth.

Then he walked away, with the wads of banknotes in his pocket.

Something similar had happened to him once before, a few years earlier, with a purse containing two hundred francs which he had found at the entrance to the Solférino Métro station. Somebody had seen him pick it up. He had had no alternative but to hand it over to the police. The station had been practically next door, and on that occasion the Mouse had not had any time to think. Instead of taking one of the notes (he was justifiably afraid of being searched) he had added a ten-franc coin. A woman came along and claimed her property.

'Describe the purse to me,' the station clerk had said to her.

The description was, of course, accurate.

'Can you tell me what it contains?'

Here, inevitably, the woman had been ten francs out. The clerk had nearly refused to return the purse to her, but in the end he had decided to do so, and the Mouse had been out of pocket as a result.

That unsuccessful attempt had taught him a lesson. As for simply keeping the wallet, there was no question of that: a man who for ten years has spent every night in a police station cannot suddenly acquire a fortune of a hundred and fifty thousand francs without being asked a certain number of indiscreet questions.

It was still raining, and the Mouse went into the Métro station at the Rond-Point, his eyes shiftier than ever, anxious not to lose a second and not to make the slightest mistake.

Since he had seen the notes, he had thought of nothing but his presbytery, the old deconsecrated presbytery of his village, which, with time, had come to represent for him the only possible refuge for his old age.

He left the Métro at Saint-Lazare. For a moment he had thought of stealing a wallet, which was not difficult, for in the cells, on crowded days, you can find yourself lying beside a pickpocket just as easily as beside a murderer, and you learn quite a few things.

Should he slip the dollars into a wallet belonging to somebody else and hand the lot into Lost Property?

No. That was dangerous and now he knew where he was going, walking faster than before. It wasn't for nothing that he had sometimes scavenged about in dustbins . . .

In the morning it would have been easy: all the dustbins there on the pavement were at your disposal.

But at ten o'clock at night . . .

He remembered a sort of cul-de-sac, off the Rue Saint-Lazare, the Avenue du Coq as it is called. There is nothing there but offices, mostly of insurance companies. A quiet avenue, without a soul about, where the dustbins are put out as early as nine o'clock in the evening.

He arrived in time. Failing a wallet, he had to have an envelope. That was his idea. And even, if possible, a rubber band.

In the dustbin he found some old envelopes bearing addresses, but he ended up by laying his hand on a yellow envelope, scarcely crumpled, which had been thrown in the waste-paper basket after a clerk had done some sums on it in pencil.

He was very keen on his rubber band. In his opinion it would make everything seem more natural. In front of the station he went into a bar and walked over to a glass case from which, for a one-franc piece, you could extract an object by means of a mechanical crane.

He had five francs left in his pocket. After putting three francs into the machine he had still not been able to get hold of the cigarette-case with a red rubber band round it.

He obtained it only with the fourth franc, ran towards the Métro, threw the cigarette-case away, and seven minutes later got out at the corner of the Rue Royale.

He had no time to worry about the fellow in the car. He was dead after all. In front of Maxim's he pretended to open a few car doors and then to pick up the yellow envelope, taking care to have Jean as a witness . . .

In the Place de la Madeleine he noticed Léa on a café terrace, under the streaming awning. At the same time he caught sight of a young policeman he did not know, and the trick was decided on. He went up to Léa and asked her:

'You haven't four francs you could lend me to take a taxi, have you?'

The young policeman fell into the trap.

'What are *you* up to?'

'I'm asking Léa for four francs . . .'

'You got any papers on you? . . . Come along with me to the station.'

The Mouse was as proud as if he had planned for this moment all his life. However much he examined all his words and actions, one by one, he could not find the smallest mistake, the slightest slip.

He could now claim to be the owner of the presbytery of Bischwiller-sur-Moder where he had not set foot for forty years.

For, after all, who could possibly claim the notes, whose number was no longer the same, and which were contained not in a wallet but in a yellow envelope with a rubber band round it?

He would wait for a year and a day, that was all. After which the chief-inspector in person would put him in legal possession of his fortune.

He was so sure of this that he occasionally found himself thinking:

'I only hope that the dollar doesn't drop in value before then!'

Then, all of a sudden, in the morning, in front of the newspaper in the window, he had had a terrible shock: there was not a single word about the fellow in the car.

What could the explanation be?

He was sure he hadn't made a mistake. He knew it was ten yards at the most beyond the British Embassy. Women in light-coloured dresses and nursemaids piloting well-dressed children were walking past.

What had become of the car?

He made for the Cours la Reine, where he strolled through the clumps of greenery.

There he had his second unpleasant surprise that day. As in the case of the car, he had imagined that it would be easy to locate the spot where he had buried the wallet.

He walked along with a casual air, for a municipal gardener was playing a hosepipe on the lawns.

However, as he walked along, his face darkened. He could not find his bearings. In the morning sunshine the scene seemed entirely different. He looked for the gas lamp which he had chosen as a landmark, and he found three similar gas lamps in front of three beds of tulips which were identical in everything except colour: there was a yellow bed, a red bed, and a mauve bed.

Only, the previous night, he had not bothered about the colour. He didn't think it was the bed of yellow tulips. But in the dark, the red and mauve tulips made the same sort of impression.

Something else worried him: the tulips were beginning to fade, and he knew what was going to happen: some carts would bring along some other flowers which would be planted in their place.

He thought fit to limp as he went over to the gardener.

'The rain last night doesn't seem to have done them any good.'

'Oh, considering how much longer they're going to stay here . . .'

'Are they going to be changed today?'

'Tomorrow morning . . .'

This was the time when the chief-inspector of the Opera district was reading the night's reports and came across the passage referring to the find made outside Maxim's of a yellow envelope containing . . .

'Send it to Lost Property,' he said to his secretary, who clipped a slip of paper to the envelope.

Chapter Two
The Portrait in the
Bowler Hat

What made the Mouse wake up with a start was the certainty which came to him through his sleep that he had not been dreaming. At the same time as that certainty and at the same time as he opened his eyes, he recognized from a combination of unpleasant sensations that he had drunk too much red wine the previous evening.

Never mind! With an effort, he sat up on the plank bed, looked for a moment at the young man who was sleeping beside him with his mouth open, and tried to recognize through the bars the women in the cage opposite.

The smell did not bother him; he was used to it. It must have been about six o'clock in the morning, for a ray of sunshine, coming in through a skylight and crossing the grey atmosphere of the station, reminded the Mouse of the picture of the Annunciation over the high altar at Bischwiller.

He scratched his feet, as he did every morning, and the more he thought about it the more certain he was that it had indeed been Inspector Lognon that he had seen during his sleep.

At the time, he had not believed it. You could almost say that for twenty-four hours he had been living with the picture of Inspector Grumpy. It was scarcely surprising, then, that his bony face with the bushy eyebrows should come and haunt him during the night.

Now the Mouse remembered half-opening lazy eyelids, thinking vaguely that he ought to make an effort to wake up, but not feeling up to it.

Another idea struck him and he turned round, frowning, as he noticed that his hat had disappeared.

So much the worse for him! It was his fault, and not simply the fault of the red wine.

As happened to him every time that he was going to do something stupid, he had had an intuition of it, the day before, about five or six o'clock, and as happened every time he had taken no notice. Because, of course, he had thought himself too clever.

How had he come to feel certain that Lognon was taking an active interest in him? It was difficult to explain. It was one of those things which you just feel. About midday, for example, when he had finally found the wallet under the tulips in the Cours la Reine, he was sure that nobody had seen him. Lognon was not yet on his track.

The Mouse had nearly given in to the temptation to take a little hundred-franc note. But no! He was too well known to do that. He would scarcely have changed the note before the news would have been known throughout the Eighth and Ninth Arrondissements, between the Étoile, the Opera and the Faubourg Montmartre.

A film-star cannot walk along a street unnoticed; still less a man like the Mouse. Every policeman in the districts he frequents knows him. So do the prostitutes and, generally speaking, all those who are to be seen in police stations. They greet each other as they pass. At night, when the Mouse arrived at the station, there was always a sergeant there to ask him:

'What were you up to at three o'clock, at the corner of the Rue Boissy-d'Anglas?'

He had not taken the hundred francs. So far, he had been cautious, and afterwards too. All that he had taken from the wallet was the little photograph, and on the back, to remember it, he had pencilled the name on the envelope: Sir Archibald Landsburry.

The weather was superb. The old man could have gone to sleep on the banks of the Seine, lulled by the panting of the crane which was unloading blocks of stone, but he had not done so.

From the wallet he had also taken the three red tickets, which were not cinema tickets but entrance tickets to Luna Park.

As he limped along with a casual air, he was thinking hard, and his first idea was to get rid of the wallet by throwing it into the Seine. He hadn't the heart to do so. It hurt him to part like that for ever with a five-hundred-dollar note and a hundred-dollar note, not to mention the French banknotes.

The fact remained that he was in danger, that the first policeman he saw, the one he noticed at the corner of the Rue Marbeuf, for example, could take it into his head to run him in, on principle, and at the station, again on principle, or out of habit, to search him.

Should he hide the wallet on a building site? An inspiration came to him as an old bus passed near him, with a man on the running-board shouting into a megaphone:

'Longchamp, two francs! . . . Longchamp . . .'

Till then he had not put a foot wrong either. He had taken a seat at the back of the bus, which he knew well, for he often went to work at the race meetings. He had made sure that the worn imitation-leather seat was not removable. Then he had pushed the wallet as far as it would go, between the seat and the back, and so as not to waste any time, he had got out at the Porte Maillot, opposite Luna Park.

Before going in, he had pushed caution to the point of slipping the photograph under the leather of his bowler hat, and he had chatted amiably with the man at the turnstile who was dressed in a splendid red uniform.

That was not dangerous. Nor was there any danger in showing him the tickets. Nor in asking casually:

'Aren't they valid any more?'

'Can't you see that they've already been used?'

'When?'

The three tickets had been used the day before, in other words on Wednesday, 23 June, in other words a few hours before the incident with the car. The Mouse discovered something else too: one of the three tickets was a half-price ticket, which had been used for a child under six years of age.

This was the time that Inspector Lognon came on duty. The Mouse knew this, and when, later on, he walked down the Champs-Élysées again, he had a distinct impression that something was happening.

This was the intuition which he had made the mistake of ignoring. He could not have said definitely what was unusual. A policeman, for example, suddenly turned round as he passed. Twice in one hour, he caught sight of the same policeman, and some distance from his station.

Now he understood, but too late. He knew how it worked. Lognon, attached to the Ninth Arrondissement, had nothing to do with the Eighth, but he could always pay his colleagues a visit, as a neighbour, and say to them:

'By the way . . . try and keep a check on the Mouse's movements . . .'

So that by giving instructions to all the policemen in the district, they could find out to the nearest minute exactly how he was spending his time.

At nine o'clock he had 'worked' the entrance to a cinema on the Champs-Élysées where there was a première in full evening dress. He had picked up twelve francs and he had spent them on drink: two whole litres, with some sausage and a loaf of fancy bread.

Then, in order to avoid Lognon, he had decided not to sleep at the Opera, but at the Grand Palais. As far as comfort went, it was exactly the same; the atmosphere was the same too. And he was just as popular in one place as in the other.

He therefore put on his usual act, with all the more verve in that there was a rather pretty young woman there. She had lost a little dog and was describing it to the sergeant. Meanwhile, a policeman felt the old man's pockets and made him take off his jacket, and the Mouse, by way of a joke and in order to amuse the young woman, had made as if to take off his trousers as well, revealing his underpants as far as his knees.

Lognon had caught him out all the same. It served him right. The inspector had come along during the night. He had discovered that nothing had been found in the old man's clothes and he had thought of the hat.

The Mouse, who was thirsty, made a noise for a good five minutes, and finally somebody came along to open the cage. The day shift had taken over from the night shift.

'I want my hat back,' he muttered.

They did not know what he was talking about. They hunted around. They found the hat behind the desk, and the Mouse put it on his head and went out.

It was only on the banks of the Seine that he took it off, found the portrait in its place, but spotted a pin-hole in the piece of cardboard.

In other words, Lognon had had the photograph copied.

Henceforth, there was a score to be settled between the two of them. The Mouse knew his Lognon like the back of his hand.

From the administrative point of view, even if the Inspector had learnt something, it was no business of his. He belonged to the municipal police. It was his job, in the Ninth Arrondissement and nowhere else, to supervise the public highway and in particular to prevent clandestine prostitution.

Even if he had discovered a crime, his role was limited

to reporting it to his superiors, who in their turn would report it to Police Headquarters.

Only, as the Mouse could tell, this was a personal matter. Lognon did not like the old tramp. Lognon hated eccentrics and he could not take a joke. Lognon had gone pale and narrowed his nostrils the day the old man had given him the nickname of Inspector Grumpy.

What was more, he was stubborn. It had taken him over twelve years to obtain the title of inspector, on account of his spelling, which resulted in his failing every examination. Three times since then he had sat the examination for the rank of chief-inspector, and the third time they had had to explain to him that his efforts were in vain, for want of a few years' extra schooling in his youth.

The fact remained that he could reel off all the regulations by heart, and that never, in matters of duty, would he compromise an iota. On the contrary, he would be stricter than ever. Without any hatred, but without any pity either, because he considered that he was paid for that.

The Mouse spent a disappointing day looking for him under a hot sun in airless streets which smelt of melting tar.

Twice he went to the Opera station where Lognon often looked in between his rounds, and didn't find him. Usually you couldn't stroll along the main boulevards at certain times of day without meeting him, staring hard at female passers-by whose progress was too slow for his liking. This time there was no Lognon. And not a word in the papers about a certain car, or about a certain person in a dinner jacket or tails who, when all was said and done, had died a violent death two days before, in the Avenue Gabriel.

Did that mean that it was one of those cases which are so important that they are made State secrets? Curiously enough, as time went by, it seemed to the Mouse that the man's face was becoming less vague in his memory.

He could not have said if the car had been standing near a gas lamp. At the time he had not paid attention to anything, but a few details had come back to him and, above all, the general appearance of the unknown man, who had been rather fat and so fair-haired that now he would have sworn that he was a foreigner. At the moment he had opened the door, the wallet must have been on his knees or on the floor of the car, for it had fallen by itself. And . . .

Nobody could have guessed that the Mouse was deep in thought. He limped along with his rather comical walk, his head bent as usual, his left foot dragging, and he did not miss a single cigarette end, even though his thoughts were elsewhere. A question of habit . . .

How could he be certain, for example, that the dead man was alone in the car when he had opened the door?

That was as far as his thoughts had taken him, and it seemed to him that he was getting warm, as children put it. The body had not been very cold yet. It had not been stiff either, but soft, almost limp.

Suppose that the man was at the wheel . . . There was somebody behind him, at the back of the car . . . The car stopped at a specific address: why not opposite the British Embassy where perhaps there was a reception?

At that moment, the man at the back bent forward, put his arms round his companion, and thrust a knife into his chest. Why a knife? The Mouse didn't know, but he imagined a knife, not even considering the possibility of a revolver.

The murderer was going to grab the wallet when he heard a dragging step, the Mouse's in fact, and he just had time to crouch down on the floor of the car.

The Mouse broke out into a slight retrospective sweat. He even began to wonder whether he hadn't heard a sound like breathing in the back of the car.

Once the Mouse had gone, the murderer came round

to the front, installed himself at the wheel, and drove the car somewhere else, to a safer place where perhaps he looked for the wallet which he had not seen fall . . .

On the café terraces, a lot of cloudy beers were being drunk, and the Mouse threaded his way between people's legs to pick up his cigarette ends, occasionally spotting a kind face and trotting out his little speech, after making sure that there was no uniform to be seen in the vicinity.

'You couldn't give me a couple of francs for a beer, could you, Your Highness?'

A knowing wink at the same time, and it was unusual for the customer not to pay up.

At eight o'clock there was still no sign of Lognon, but a little later, when the old man was sitting down on a kerb, near the Opera station, to have a snack, he caught sight of the inspector's brown suit. Lognon had seen him too, that was certain. However, contrary to his habit, and instead of telling him to move on somewhere else, he quickened his pace, turning his head away as if he did not want to be recognized.

It was the Mouse who had to run after him, something which was far from easy. The nearer he got to him, the faster the other man walked, and finally he had to call out to him.

'Hey! . . . Inspector! . . . Wait for me, damn it! . . . I've got something to tell you . . .'

This time Lognon stopped short, showing an impassive face in which the eyebrows seemed thicker than ever.

'What have you got to tell me?'

'Nothing at all.'

'Well then?'

He was going to go off again!

'Hang on a minute, for God's sake! I want to tell you something all the same . . . But you mustn't hustle me like that . . .'

He no longer knew how to set about it. The two of them

were standing there near the stage-door. The evening was calm, the sky a soft pink.

'Speak up!' said Lognon impatiently.

'It's about the little lady . . .'

This was followed by a wink and an embarrassed look.

'I'm listening.'

'You know whom I'm talking about, don't you?'

'I'm waiting for you to tell me.'

'Listen . . . You're more intelligent than I am, and it isn't fair to take advantage of that. Exchange is no robbery . . . I play fair, I do . . . You tell me something and I'll tell you something too . . .'

At moments like this the Mouse had an innocent, child-like look. He knew it. He played with his wrinkled old face like an artist.

'Speak up, anyway . . .'

'No. You know that the Mouse always keeps his word . . . If you give me a piece of information, I'll give you one, which might be important.'

'Come along to the station . . .'

'I'd rather talk here. Besides, at the station, your colleagues would hear me, and you wouldn't be the only one to benefit . . .'

He saw that the other man was hesitating, that he was tempted.

'What do you know?'

'If you answer my question, I'll tell you.'

'All right then, ask your question.'

'Where does the little lady live?'

The inspector was taking the matter very seriously, thinking it over, and giving the old man sidelong glances.

'What little lady?'

'You know. Mind you, I'm capable of finding her too, but I haven't got the same facilities as you have. For instance, I'm sure you've been to see all the photographers

who do that sort of portrait . . . Just think of the time that
would take me with my old legs! . . . Not to mention the
fact that you can get your colleagues to help you . . .'

Lognon looked away, anxious, in spite of everything,
to find out what he could.

'What are you going to tell me? Let's walk along,
people are looking at us . . .'

'Do you want me to pretend to be asking you for
money?'

He did this, but with an anxious look in his eyes.

'Inspector, you've got a kind heart. Take pity on a poor
man who wants to find a lost child.'

'What's that you're saying? Is she your daughter?'

'I didn't say that . . .'

He mustn't make another slip. The fish was nibbling.
Lognon had almost made up his mind.

'An old beggar like the Mouse can sometimes render
important service . . . I can tell that you've found her . . .
Don't deny it! . . . You're too honest for that.'

'You speak first then.'

'That wouldn't be fair . . . But I give you my word that
I will tell you something . . . Where does she live?'

'In the Avenue du Parc-Montsouris . . .'

'Towards the Belfort Lion or towards the Park?'

'Near the Rue Dareau . . . Now, speak up! Why did you
hide that photograph in your hat? On Wednesday night,
when you were searched at the station, it wasn't there . . .
Where did you get it?'

'I found it.'

Lognon gave him a stern look, as if to say that the time
for joking had passed.

'Who was it that wrote a name on the back?'

'You know perfectly well, seeing that you know my
handwriting. It was me.'

'Why?'

'Because I had a pencil . . .'

'Come along with me to the station.'

At the entrance to the Opera, a policeman on duty looked at them in amusement, wondering what had brought the tramp and Inspector Grumpy to grips once more. The latter noticed and nearly lost his temper.

'Come along with me!'

'Just a minute . . . I'll talk, honest I will . . .'

'Where did you get that name?'

'Archibald Landsburry?' recited the Mouse.

'Where did you get it?'

'I read it on the registration plate of a car . . .'

He was playing for time . . .

'Where was that?'

'In front of the Taverne Royale . . .'

'And why did you make a note of it?'

'Because I wanted to say a prayer for the person in the car, who had given me a five-franc tip . . .'

'Was it a man?'

'Yes.'

'Middle-aged?'

'Yes . . . with his hair going grey . . .'

The Mouse was beginning to feel worried. He wondered why the inspector was going full tilt after a name instead of inquiring about the girl in the photograph.

'When was this?'

'Yesterday, about four o'clock.'

What if Archibald Landsburry turned out to be the man in the car, the corpse of the Avenue Gabriel?

'And the photograph?'

'I found it . . .'

'In the street, just like that, by accident?'

'No. On the floor, in a bar in the Rue . . . in the Rue Washington . . .'

The Mouse was beginning to feel really frightened.

There was no longer any hope of gaining time by playing the fool and Lognon asked in a harsh voice:

'Now, what did you want to tell me?'

His gaze gave the Mouse to understand that if he was not satisfied the consequences could be serious.

'I wanted to tell you that I met the lady in the photograph the day before yesterday, yes, on the twenty-third in the afternoon, at Luna Park . . .'

'Go on.'

'There's nothing more . . . She was with a little boy and a gentleman . . .'

'You saw her?'

'Yes . . .'

'What was the man like?'

He had to talk to find out.

'A man with fair hair . . . Very fair hair . . . rather fat . . .'

Now this reply seemed to calm the Inspector down. So it didn't contradict his own information in any way. To salve his conscience, he growled:

'What were you doing at Luna Park?'

'You know perfectly well . . . They sometimes need a hand with some side-show or other . . . Now and then I'm asked to beat the drum, and even, on days when a musician's missing, to play the horn . . .'

On Lognon's face, as severely carved as a wooden head, you could distinguish the effort of thought, the fear of being fooled, the determination to be right, to arrive at a solution.

'Is that all that you know?'

'What else could I know?' retorted the Mouse with admirably simulated innocence.

'Yes, of course,' the other man's expression seemed to say.

And yet he was unhappy about letting go. It seemed to him that he was not up to his task, that it only needed a very little, a gleam of light, to discover something which he could only suspect.

'What are you going to do with that photo?'

'And you?'

'That's my business.'

'Well, with me, seeing that feelings are involved, it's even more private. You aren't going to forbid me to be in love, are you?'

'You haven't seen the last of me,' said the inspector menacingly, turning away.

But he stopped again, and made a last attempt.

'You've made up your mind, have you?'

'What about?'

It was no use pressing the point. It was better to go home and think about it all.

As for the Mouse, he went to spend the night at the Central Market station, which was on the way to the Avenue du Parc-Montsouris. It wasn't as clean as the Opera, and there was a smell of vegetables in the air. He didn't know anybody either; but he was lucky enough to come across an old man who had a whole parcel of scraps of food and who went shares with him.

Just before going to sleep, the Mouse had asked his neighbour, who was busy scratching a corn with his penknife:

'You don't happen to know an Archibald Landsburry, do you?'

'Never heard of him,' the other man had retorted.

Lognon, for his part, had only had to open a social directory, after reading the name on the back of the photograph, to make sure that he was not mistaken and that this was indeed the name of the British Ambassador in Paris. There was only one mistake: on the photograph the name was preceded by Sir, and the Ambassador was a Lord.

As for finding the original of the photograph, that had

been far easier, contrary to all expectations. Lognon, that afternoon, had got a colleague in the Ninth Arrondissement to take his place; then he had gone to the Quai des Orfèvres to the Criminal Records Office.

He was all the more embarrassed in that it had been his dream in the past to work in this building, the occupants of which represented, in his eyes, the aristocracy of the police force.

It was not a high-ranking official whom he asked to see, but an ordinary photographer, and he found himself up in the attics, in the presence of a thin young man with a face covered with freckles.

'Inspector Lognon of the Ninth Arrondissement . . . I must apologize for troubling you, because I'm not here on an official errand.'

At bottom Lognon was a shy man with a considerable inferiority complex.

'I'd like to ask you . . . supposing you were given this photograph and asked to find the original . . .'

'The woman?'

'Yes. Are there, for example, many cameras which take the same sort of photograph?'

'There were a lot five or six years ago . . . Now people use automatic cameras . . .'

'Well?'

Yes, well what? Wasn't a technician bound to find a solution?

'You'd have to begin by looking through the records . . . You never know . . .'

That was all. The photographer did not know anything more.

'If you start going round all the photographers in Paris,' he said half-heartedly.

Well, Lognon would do that if it was necessary. Possibly for nothing. He would spend his annual leave on it. But he would find out what was hidden behind the Mouse's mysterious behaviour.

All the same, he asked on the off chance to see an inspector in the Vice Squad, a colleague in fact, but a colleague in the Big House.

He was taken along corridor after corridor, like an ordinary member of the public. He waited in an ante-room. He had to show his photograph a dozen times, and in the end he was handed first a record card, then a file.

'Lucile Boisvin, born in the Department of Seine-et-Marne, maid of all work at a baker's in the Avenue des Ternes, arrested for the first time for clandestine prostitution on . . .'

Arrested twice, three times, seven years before, when she was eighteen. He felt in his element once more, found echoes of the style of his own reports, and took notes at random.

Lucile Boisvin had not taken long to reform, and a few months later, as a result of a report from an inspector who stated that she had a home of her own, at No. 37 Avenue du Parc-Montsouris, and that she had a regular source of income, she ceased to be the object of special supervision.

It turned out, in fact, that she had a lover, a Swiss commercial traveller called Leroy, who contributed to her maintenance.

At five o'clock, while the police of the Eighth Arrondissement were keeping an eye on the Mouse's movements, Lognon was ringing on the doorbell of a flat in the Avenue du Parc-Montsouris. It was on the sunny side of the avenue, and he was dazzled, as soon as he entered, by the brightness of the flat, with its white walls, its gaily coloured curtains, and its furniture which was so clean that it looked as if it had come straight from the shop.

A little boy of five was playing on the balcony. As for

Lucile Boisvin, who was dressed in bright colours too, she no longer recalled the unruly child in the portrait, or the police reports, but suggested rather a model young mother, knitting with green wool.

As Lognon walked in without saying anything, with his stubborn look, she gave a start and asked:

'Did Edgar send you?'

Then, frightened by the bushy eyebrows which drew together, she said:

'Nothing's happened to him, has it?'

'I don't think so . . . I found this photograph in the neighbourhood . . . I wanted to give it back to you . . .'

She didn't understand.

'How did you know it was me?'

Then, rather embarrassed, he explained that he lived in the Rue Dareau, that he had already caught sight of her, and that he had thought that this photograph might have sentimental value for her.

As for her, nonplussed, she turned the piece of cardboard over and over between her fingers.

'It *was* Edgar, wasn't it, who told you . . .'

He felt uneasy, for he was not there on official business. He was in a hurry to get away . . .

'I just don't understand . . . This looks like the photo he insisted on keeping in his pocket . . . Tell me . . . You're sure nothing has happened to him . . .'

The child was listening to them. While Lucile Boisvin was dark, the boy had silver-blond hair and a milky-white complexion.

'Why hasn't he come?' she murmured as if to herself.

This visitor intrigued her. She had not asked him to sit down. It was warm, and Lognon reflected that he would have liked a flat as light as this one, without a single object lying around, without a single speck of dust, a flat which, in fact, made him think of a luxury clinic.

'Were you expecting Monsieur Leroy?' he asked clumsily.

'You see – you *do* know him! Tell me quickly what you've got to say . . .'

'I assure you . . . I found the photo . . . I asked at the dairy shop where you lived . . .'

'But how do you know my lover's name?'

She said 'lover' naturally, without any false modesty, without bothering about the child.

'It was the concierge . . .'

'Ah!'

She did not believe him. But she did not know how to set about making him talk, and she let him back out of the flat, listened to him walking down the three flights of stairs instead of taking the lift, put the photograph on the table and stayed for quite a while gazing anxiously at it.

At a certain moment she turned it over automatically, saw the name of Sir Archibald Landsburry, and shrugged her shoulders as if to say:

'Well, we'll see . . .'

She had never heard anybody mention that name and she scarcely ever read the newspapers.

Chapter Three
Monsieur Frédéric Müller and
Dora the Hungarian

They were two horrible hours – horrible is not too strong
a word for them – but of a horror devoid of grandeur or
poetry, two hours begun in an uneasiness which gradually
turned into panic, in that huge drawing-room where he had
to remain motionless at all costs under the gaze of seven
or eight people who for their part seemed entirely at their
ease.

Time and again, Lognon nearly stood up and asked for
his brown hat back from the valet who had taken it from
him, something that had added still further to his discom-
fiture, for he was used to waiting with his hat on his
knees.

He scarcely entered the British Embassy, before he re-
gretted doing so and started looking enviously through the
windows at the free foliage of the trees in the avenue.

In any case, he had been wrong. He was always wrong
to want to do things too well, as his wife wore herself out
repeating to him.

That he should feel an urge to clear up the mystery
surrounding the envelope with the dollars and show the
Mouse that a police inspector was not necessarily a fool was
only natural.

Only this time, he had gone rather far. Sending his card
in to Lord Archibald Landsburry, the British Ambassador!
His process-engraved card which bore the words: 'Inspector of the Municipal Police'. Visitors kept coming
into the drawing-room and either remained standing or sat

down, but none of them so far had stayed there more than twenty minutes.

After an hour, Lognon was sweating with anguish. Then he convinced himself that the ambassador had telephoned to the Prefect to complain of this impertinent intrusion.

Finally, all of a sudden, he had been shown into a luxurious office, where an affected young man had offered him a chair.

'Lord Landsburry?' had stammered Lognon, whose eyes grew wilder the more embarrassed he became.

'One of his secretaries . . .'

'But it's Lord Landsburry himself that . . .'

What happened next, he could not have said. He crossed two offices, went through a padded door, found himself in a room of hitherto unsuspected majesty, and plunged towards a seated personage, towards a monocle.

'I simply wanted to ask Your Excellency if you know this person . . .'

And he produced the photograph of Lucile Boisvin, of which, while he was about it, he had had half a dozen copies printed. It was all he had at his disposal, and he had decided that he might as well use it.

The ambassador was so astonished by the question that he stared at the photograph for quite a while before handing it back to the inspector.

'Who is it?' he asked at last.

'Nobody . . . It doesn't matter . . . Seeing that you don't know her . . .'

He left without his hat. The footman had to run after him to give it back to him. He felt humiliated, squashed, and peeved all at once. And he was frightened too into the bargain, for his card had remained on Lord Landsburry's desk, and the ambassador, to salve his conscience, could easily get somebody to telephone the Prefecture.

Now, coming out of the Embassy, he had scarcely started

walking towards the opposite pavement before he noticed, peacefully installed on a bench, the old Mouse.

Lognon did not take the trouble to think. He advanced on the old man with such a determined air that the tramp raised his arm as if to ward off a blow.

'What are you doing here?'

'You can see for yourself, I'm eating. And you? Tell me, what did Archibald have to say?'

The uniformed porter standing at the door of the Embassy could see them. Lognon was becoming peevish, for he felt that he was allowing himself to be drawn into an imprudent course of action.

'Listen . . . The two of us have got to have a chat . . . Will you come to my place tonight, about eight o'clock? It's number twenty-nine, Place . . .'

'Constantin-Pecqueur . . . I know!'

And the Mouse winked, walked away, dragging his left leg.

At eight o'clock, when the door-bell of the flat rang, Lognon motioned to his wife, who grabbed her son by the arm, and took him into the bedroom, closing the door behind them. At the same time, the inspector, on his way to open the door, switched off the wireless which was playing quietly.

Everything was more or less tidy. They had had dinner a little earlier on purpose. One of the boy's exercise books and an arithmetic book were lying open on the table. On the sideboard there were some plums left over from the meal.

The Mouse came in looking as if he did not know exactly what was waiting for him, and, putting on his little act, looked around him and gave a whistle.

'I say! It isn't at all bad, where you live!'

There wasn't much room, that was the worst of it. It

was a small room. You could only just get between the pieces of furniture, but with an orange lampshade in iridescent glass, it was cosy.

Lognon had kept his slippers on.

'Sit down.'

An unpleasant feeling, which resembled the panic he had felt at the Embassy, came over him, and he chose his words carefully, terrified at the idea of committing a blunder and above all endangering his job.

It seemed to him that his visitor too was nervous, even feverish, that his gaze was unusually steady, but he made the mistake of putting this down to the Mouse's awe at being received for the first time in his life in a police inspector's flat.

'We're going to have a serious chat, eh?' he said, filling a pipe which he smoked only at home.

He made an effort to smile.

'All open and above board, eh?'

When he repeated 'eh . . . eh' like that it meant that he was unsure of himself, and this time he went on repeating it again and again.

'Cards on the table, eh?'

He did not see that the old man's hands, hidden by the fringed table-cloth, were trembling on his knees.

For if, on 24 June, 25 June, and the morning of the 26th there had not been a word in the papers about the car and the dead man, the Mouse, barely an hour before, had read in an evening paper:

DISQUIETING DISAPPEARANCE
OF SWISS FINANCIER IN PARIS

The police have just been notified of the mysterious disappearance of a leading figure in the world of finance, Monsieur Edgar Loëm of Basle.

Monsieur Loëm, who is the presiding genius of a financial organization known as the Basle Group made frequent stays in the various capitals of Europe and particularly in Paris.

Here he had rented, by the year, a suite in the Hôtel Castiglione, on the corner of the Place Vendôme, where Monsieur Frédéric Müller, his agent for the French branches of the group, also resides.

Finally – a detail which is not without importance – whenever Monsieur Loëm was in our capital, he would hire a limousine from a garage near the Étoile, which he used to drive himself.

It was in this car that on 23 June, about eight o'clock, he left the Place Vendôme, and he was probably going to some reception, for he was wearing tails.

It should be noted that Monsieur Loëm, who was known only in certain financial circles, was a very quiet man, whose social life was reduced to the strict minimum.

Where was he going that evening? He did not tell his agent Müller. The fact remains that the next day, he had not returned to the Hôtel Castiglione. And today, 26 June, there is still no news of him.

Up to the very last moment, Monsieur Müller thought that, as sometimes happened, the financier had travelled to Brussels or Amsterdam without giving any warning. But telephone calls made to his various homes give reason to suppose that Monsieur Loëm's absence is not voluntary.

The hired car, which was recently bought second-hand by the garage from a manufacturer in Seine-et-Oise, still carried its own registration number: Y.A. 5–6713. It is a dark-blue six seater saloon.

As for Monsieur Loëm, he is a short man with very fair hair. He has a slight foreign accent, and a tendency to corpulence.

According to Monsieur Frédéric Müller, he was not in the habit of carrying large sums about on him.

The case has been entrusted to Chief-Inspector Lucas of Police Headquarters.

An hour before reading this news-item, the Mouse would have given a great deal to have done with uncertainty, to know at last the identity of his corpse. He had genuinely been looking forward to his conversation with the inspector in his flat, and he had limped gaily in the direction of Montmartre.

It was at the tobacconist's in the Place Clichy that he had read the paper, and since then he had been trying in vain to recover his composure.

'Have a cigarette?' Lognon asked him in a gruff voice.

'I don't mind if I do . . .'

Madame Lognon, in the next room, was putting the boy to bed: people could be heard moving about on the floor above. Lognon took his time in putting on a severe expression, and lowered his brows before bringing his gaze to bear on the tramp.

'You want to play fair with me, eh?'

Once again that 'eh' which betrayed him.

'Listen . . . You know me . . . You know that I won't let go of you before knowing what I want to know . . .'

'I know you,' admitted the Mouse.

'There are colleagues of mine who, if they were in my place, would set about it in a different way.'

The old man gave a slight smile. Threats did not frighten him. He knew that the inspector was referring to an arrest on some charge, imaginary or otherwise, such as can always be brought against a tramp.

The pipe was dirty and made an unpleasant little noise, but Lognon must have been used to it, for he did not notice it.

'I'm not telling you, either, that if you've got something on your conscience I'll see that you're all right. That isn't my way . . .'

That was true. He was an honest man at bottom. And indeed, deep down, a good sort.

Only, the trouble was that he wanted to find out.

'Answer honestly. That's the best thing for you to do . . .'

'Answer who?' said the tramp, playing the innocent.

'Me!'

'I beg your pardon. Have I to answer Inspector Lognon of the Ninth Arrondissement, or Monsieur Joseph Lognon of 29 Place Constantin-Pecqueur? That's what I'd like to know . . .'

Obviously! He had made a mistake in inviting the old man to his home.

'Answer whoever you like. First of all, tell me how you got to know that woman . . .'

'Lucile Boisvin?' the Mouse asked calmly.

'You see, you know her all right!'

'Like you . . . and only since today . . . You were kind enough to tell me last night that she lived in the Avenue du Parc-Montsouris . . . This morning I went there and I sat down on the same bench as her while the little boy was playing in the park . . .'

'Did you speak to her?'

'Not on the bench! It isn't done to speak to a woman in the street. I waited until she'd gone home, after doing her shopping in the Avenue d'Orléans . . . Two mutton chops, that's what she bought . . .'

'You went to her flat?'

'To give her the photo back like you . . . She gave me a horrified look and then she went to get another photo just like it from the mantelpiece. She couldn't make head or tail of it . . .'

'What did she say to you?'

'She asked me if I knew Monsieur Leroy . . . She was trembling . . . At one moment, I wondered if she wasn't going to burst into tears . . . As for me, I told her straight out that I'd never heard of Monsieur Leroy, but that there was a name written on the back of the photo . . . You know . . . Archibald . . .'

'And then?'

'That's all, I thought it best to push off . . . it was just after

44

coming out that I got the idea of looking for Archibald Landsburry in the social directory . . . Only I can't walk into an Embassy like some people . . . What did our Archibald say to you?'

'Nothing.'

Lognon had spoken without thinking. He corrected himself.

'That's no business of yours.'

'You see what you're like! I tell you everything, I do, straight out, because I've got nothing to hide . . . Lord, but it's hellish hot here.'

And he wiped his forehead with his sleeve. Then he stood up.

'You can see that we've got nothing more to say to each other.'

'Mosselbach!' said Lognon, using this name for the first time.

'Well?'

'Tell me the truth!'

'What truth?'

'The business of the dollars and the photo . . .'

'You want me to start all over again? Well, here goes! It was Wednesday, and I'd gone to have some soup on the Salvation Army barge, seeing that Wednesday's my day. It was raining, and . . .'

'That's not what I'm asking you.'

For he was lying. Lognon could feel it. He had felt it from the very first day, from the clown-like entrance the Mouse had made at the Opera station. And his suspicions had been increased by all those details of time and place, by the commissionaire at Maxim's, by Léa, by the story of the four francs for a taxi . . .

'If you insist, I can make things up . . . I'm a regular artist at that. Let's say I stole the banknotes from a drunken customer . . .'

'That's enough!'

It was best to leave it at that. Lognon would have been capable of doing something silly. He walked over to the door and opened it.

'We'll see,' he said in a threatening voice.

'If that's all you asked me to come here for . . . Good-bye all the same . . . If you need me again, you can find me at the station any time after midnight . . .'

And going down the three flights of stairs, the Mouse muttered:

'Loëm . . . Loëm . . . He was called Loëm . . .'

And what of it? What could it matter to him, now that he came to think of it?

At noon the next day, when he left the office of the local chief-inspector, Lognon had unburdened his conscience. It was better that way. Besides, the chief-inspector had listened to him without much interest, had said: 'Hmm . . . Hmm . . .' several times, and finally had declared:

'Put all that down on paper for me . . . I'll send a report in just in case . . . But seeing that there hasn't been any complaint . . .'

He tried to write the report in his office, stopped four or five times after a few lines, and finally went off to work at home.

It was terribly difficult. With the spoken word he could still manage to communicate his suspicions, or at least to make them plausible. In writing, it was all reduced to the level of idle gossip.

'. . . it is certain that the attitude adopted by the Mouse, whom I have known for ten years . . .'

'. . . it is clear that the action of hiding this photograph under the leather of his hat . . .'

'. . . it seems obvious that if somebody had really lost over 150,000 francs on 23 June, he would have made himself known by now . . .'

He read his report to his wife, who was not very well and scarcely listened.

'What do you think of it?'

'I think that you ought not to invite people like that here . . . You never know . . .'

Once the report had been deposited on the chief-inspector's desk, he felt a sense of relief all the same. He promised himself, in order to change his ideas, to make a more extensive tour that night, into the most out-of-the-way corners of the district, and he firmly resolved to steer clear of the Mouse, so as to avoid all temptation.

DRAMATIC NEW DEVELOPMENT IN
THE CASE OF THE SWISS FINANCIER
A YOUNG HUNGARIAN WOMAN
ACCUSES FRÉDÉRIC MÜLLER
OF MURDERING HIS CHIEF

Last night we reported the disappearance, since 23 June, of the Swiss financier Edgar Loëm, who had left the Hôtel Castiglione about eight o'clock to go to a reception. Let us remind our readers that it was Monsieur Loëm's agent in France, Frédéric Müller, who was the first to notify the police of his suspicions.

This morning Chief-Inspector Lucas, of Police Headquarters, went to the Hôtel Castiglione to obtain information necessary for his inquiries.

The Hôtel Castiglione, although situated on the corner of the street of the same name and the Place Vendôme, is not an aggressively luxurious establishment. On the ground floor it has just a revolving door between the shop windows of a furrier and a famous picture dealer.

The atmosphere is severe and just a little old-fashioned. A staircase with bronze torch-holders and a crimson carpet leads to the first floor, where the drawing-rooms and the offices are situated.

As for the clientele, it consists chiefly of regular patrons, especially foreign businessmen who prefer peace and quiet to ostentatious luxury.

The maître d'hôtel, who has been at the hotel for forty years, gave us quite a vivid description of Monsieur Edgar Loëm, whom he called the simplest and most discreet of men. He added:

'People who didn't know him could easily have taken him for a cashier or a bank clerk. He was nearly always dressed in grey, his favourite colour. As he always occupied the same suite, he had it likewise papered in grey.'

He had no office. This was to be found in Monsieur Müller's suite, which communicated with his own. In principle, Monsieur Loëm was not at home to anybody and never answered the telephone.

It was Monsieur Müller who received callers. Sometimes he would leave his visitor for a moment, to go into the next room to talk to his chief.

When we put an indiscreet question to the maître d'hôtel, he protested:

'Women – Monsieur Loëm? Never, Monsieur! Neither women nor drink, nor tobacco . . .'

Finally, to complete the picture of the vanished mystery man, he gave these particulars:

'No, you couldn't say that he worked a lot. All the files were in a safe in Monsieur Müller's suite. On the other hand, he spent hours with his stamp collection.'

Let us come now to the dramatic development which occurred this morning. Chief-Inspector Lucas, who is noted for his discretion, had just spent an hour alone with Monsieur Frédéric Müller, and nothing had arisen from the conversation between the two men.

There were a few of us journalists in the hotel lounge, when a young woman of striking elegance emerged from the lift, which had come down from the upper floors.

She immediately attracted attention, not only because of her light-coloured silk suit and her mahogany-coloured hair but also because of her extreme agitation. I am convinced that, for her part, she recognized us as members of the Press, for she came straight towards us.

48

'Is he still there?' she asked, pointing to Müller's door.

Then, without waiting for the reply, she called to the maître d'hôtel who was passing:

'Germain! Bring me a cocktail straight away.'

'A pink one, Miss Dora?'

Rumanian? Hungarian? We argued for a moment in an undertone about her accent. During this time she was pacing up and down the hall, stabbing the crimson carpet with her high heels. Then she drained at one draught the contents of the glass Germain brought her on a tray.

I had time to notice that the manager and the chief receptionist seemed worried by her agitation, and were talking about it in low voices.

At the same moment, the door opened. The chief-inspector came out first followed by a thin man with a centre parting.

Chief-Inspector Lucas had not had time to shake the hand which Müller held out to him before the young woman stepped forward, declaring in a categorical voice:

'He's the man who killed Edgar!'

The excitement this caused can easily be imagined. However, Miss Dora went on in a state of feverish agitation, interspersing her remarks with a few foreign words:

'No, I'm not mad, as he will try and get you to believe . . .'
As the chief-inspector took a step in the direction of the drawing-room, she cried out even more urgently:

'These gentlemen of the Press can hear everything. I say that it's Müller who has killed Edgar Loëm . . . He probably maintains that he hasn't seen him since eight o'clock on the twenty-third, but I declare that they went off together in the car . . . The maître d'hôtel will confirm that in the morning they had a long discussion, and that Loëm raised his voice, something which never happened with him before.'

At that moment, the chief-inspector managed to get her into the drawing-room, the door of which closed. There must have been a telephone conversation with Police Headquarters, for half an hour later an examining magistrate arrived at the hotel, accompanied by his clerk, and the drawing-room door closed behind them.

Germain, the maître d'hôtel, was allowed in a little later, stayed only a few minutes, and refused to make any statement to the Press, neither confirming nor denying the allegation about the discussion between the financier and his agent.

Although we are not in a position to reveal the source of our information, we can state that Miss Dora, a young Hungarian belonging to a family of leading lawyers in Budapest (a fact which encourages us to keep her name quiet) has been installed in the Hôtel Castiglione for over a year, and that she was on close terms with Frédéric Müller.

In spite of the discretion observed by the staff of this silent establishment we believe we can assert that she was his mistress, and we know among other things that he paid her bills.

As for the results of the interview, we are reduced to supposition. At noon, Chief-Inspector Lucas and the examining magistrate left in a taxi, refusing to make any comment.

Miss Dora ran across the lounge and, scorning the lift, returned to her suite, where she locked herself in. As for Müller, who had not been arrested, it seems that he has been asked to hold himself at the disposal of the police. In any case, passing the hotel in the early afternoon, we noticed the discreet presence of an inspector from Police Headquarters.

'What are you doing there?'

'You can see for yourself, Officer. I'm not doing anything. And you?'

'Move along now.'

The Mouse shrugged his shoulders, with the look of a misunderstood man. Nobody in the Eighth or Ninth Arrondissements would ever have spoken to him in that tone. Above all, nobody would ever have asked him such a silly question. But there it was. The Place Vendôme is in the Second Arrondissement, and the Mouse, a famous figure from the Étoile to the Opera, was just an anonymous tramp outside his own realm.

Was it Saturday? Probably, because it was a motor-coach day. In the space of an hour, three stopped in front of the

Vendôme column, crammed with English people who had bought week-end tickets entitling them to a tour of Paris.

The sun was blazing down. The papers were full of photographs of the banks of the Seine, showing people wearing bathing costumes, as if they were at the seaside, under the headline: 'Heat Wave in Paris'.

No Lognon! There had been no Lognon the previous night either, even though the Mouse had slept at the Opera on purpose. And it was just as worrying not to see Inspector Grumpy as to see too much of him.

Edgar Loëm . . . Müller . . . Miss Dora . . . The Mouse knew the article by heart. It was the best one, for he had read those in the other papers and he had compared them with one another. What he would have liked most of all was to see Müller, with his centre parting, but Müller did not come out and, apart from the inspector from Police Headquarters there were two photographers walking up and down the Rue Castiglione, pretending to take an interest either in furs or in the pictures in the gallery on the corner.

All the same, one of the coaches provided the Mouse with three francs, not to mention a few pennies. He had to sheer off for quite a while, for the policeman who had been watching him from a distance had come striding across the street.

If only he had been able to change places with them all!

With Lognon, who had been able to go into the British Embassy and see the famous Archibald at close quarters. With Chief-Inspector Lucas, who had interrogated Müller and Miss Dora, and who must have rummaged among the financier's papers. Even with the journalists who could go into the Hôtel Castiglione and question the staff . . .

He, for his part, could not even go and get a little money for his petty expenses from the wallet, which, at that moment, was travelling towards the Auteuil race-course, squeezed between the back and the seat of a coach.

Nor could he, without considerable risk, go and extract

from the wallet the envelope which he had made the mistake of not examining more closely.

'Sir Archibald Landsbury . . .'

What was he doing mixed up in this affair? And why *Sir* instead of *Lord*? And why had the corpse been only a few yards from the British Embassy?

The fourth time he saw his policeman striding towards him, he decided to clear off for good. It disgusted him not to be able to have a moment's peace. He felt almost like dropping everything, seeing that in a year's time he would be claiming the one hundred and fifty thousand francs (unless the bottom dropped out of the dollar) and would be able to buy his deconsecrated presbytery.

Only, instead of going to have a rest in the shade on one of the quays of the Seine, he crossed the Pont des Arts, and then, a quarter of an hour later, the Boulevard Saint-Germain.

He dragged his left leg all the time. He did not walk fast, but he made good headway, for he never stopped.

When he reached the Belfort Lion, he was still thinking about the same thing: about the three tickets to Luna Park and about the word he had heard that morning when he had been sitting on a bench in the Montsouris Park next to Lucile Boisvin. The boy had gone off a little way and disappeared behind a clump of bushes. Without stopping knitting with her green wool, without even looking around her, accustomed, in fact, to summoning her progeny like a mother hen, she had called out:

'Edgar!'

He had paid no attention. Only since he had read the paper, and knew that Loëm too was called Edgar . . .

Now Lognon was bound to know that the child was called Edgar. Lognon read the papers . . .

He had to find some way out of the mess, some dodge or other.

Wasn't it rotten luck that in spite of all the precautions he had taken . . .

The old man walked along the Avenue du Parc-Mont-souris, on the shady side. He wanted to have a drink, but he did not dare to, for fear of meeting Lognon and being in a state of inferiority.

Not to mention the fact that, even without Lognon, if he, the Mouse, didn't think of something . . .

Naturally, the afternoon papers did not carry Loëm's photograph as yet. But it would be in the papers the next day. The papers always publish the photographs of people who have disappeared, especially in such mysterious circumstances, especially when they are financiers . . .

Lucile Boisvin would recognize her commercial traveller Leroy, who was none other than that joker Loëm. And then . . .

Why then, in spite of all his clever tricks, the Mouse would be done for. That was what he thought. That was why he refused to allow himself the smallest pernod, the smallest glass of red wine.

A week before, he wouldn't have cared. But when a man is, so to speak, the owner of a deconsecrated presbytery in his own village, at Bischwiller-sur-Moder where masses of people would recognize him and where he would become an important person . . .

Chapter Four
The Petty Accounts of a
Great Financier

It was on Sunday, 27 June, at five o'clock in the afternoon, that Chief-Inspector Lucas suddenly opened the door of the suite, with an abruptness which betrayed his anger. With a single glance, he took in that part of the lounge which was occupied by the Press, and, while the journalists' laughter froze on their lips, he uttered the famous sentence:

'You seem to be forgetting, gentlemen, that there is probably a dead man in this case.'

While he was speaking his gaze had ended up resting on the old Mouse, who was preening himself in the middle of the group, and who for a moment looked as if he were shrinking, as if he wanted to make himself smaller, to disappear into the anonymous crowd.

Still holding the handle of the door, behind which they could catch a glimpse of Edgar Loëm's suite, the chief-inspector first of all made as if to go back, then jerked his head to summon the inspector he had left in the lounge.

He murmured a few words to him, nodding in the direction of the old tramp. From the movement of his lips, it was clear that he was asking:

'What's he doing here?'

And the inspector was replying:

'He's a queer old chap who says that he's got something he wants to tell you . . .'

The Mouse did not miss a single one of the gestures or the facial expressions of the two men.

'All right. I'll see him in a minute,' said Lucas, who finally went back into the suite and shut the door.

Straight away, like schoolboys when the master has left the room, the journalists crowded round the Mouse, who in a flash, so to speak, turned back into the clown-like character who had been amusing them for half an hour, to the extent of making the chief-inspector come out into the lounge.

'Right, go on with the story of Inspector Grumpy . . .'

To the horror of the manager of the Hôtel Castiglione, some photographers climbed up on the sofas to take photographs of the tramp.

What had happened, that Sunday morning, was precisely what the Mouse had foreseen. While most of the people of Paris were setting off for the country, and the streets were assuming their peaceful Sunday appearance, Lucile Boisvin, as usual, found the newspaper on the milk-can waiting outside her door. At that time of day, the flat was so sunny that it seemed to be full of tiny particles of sunshine which blurred the outlines of things.

The boy was drinking his chocolate, with his napkin tied round his neck and his little legs not quite touching the floor. The paper could have lain around on a table until noon, or even all day. If Lucile Boisvin opened it, it was by chance, but she gave a stifled cry, turned round to glance at the child, who had not noticed anything, and ran into the bedroom to have a closer look at the photograph which was spread out on the front page.

THE FINANCIER EDGAR LOËM, WHO HAS MYSTERIOUSLY DISAPPEARED

All they had been able to find to give the Press was a photograph which was ten years old. At that time, Loëm had still been wearing a long fair moustache which made him look as if he had stepped out of the Universal Exhibition of 1900.

Lucile Boisvin none the less recognized her lover, Monsieur Leroy. Ten minutes latter she was dressed. Then she dressed the little boy, and took him down to the concierge, whom she asked to take care of him until she got back.

For the first time for years, the flat was still untidy at ten o'clock, and the breeze was puffing out the curtains like a balloon, for the windows had been left open.

Chief-Inspector Lucas was at home when the inspector on duty at the Quai de Orfèvres telephoned the news to him. He reached his office at half past ten and found half a dozen journalists in the corridor of Police Headquarters.

At noon, a paper published a photograph of the young woman and announced:

Mademoiselle Lucile Boisvin has recognized the photograph of the Swiss financier, but the latter, who was her lover, passed himself off to her as a commercial traveller of the same nationality.

This afternoon, Chief-Inspector Lucas is to take the girl to the Hôtel Castiglione to see if she can recognize any of the clothes of the vanished financier.

Monsieur Müller, who has not left his suite, saw one of the most famous barristers in Paris last night, but the latter has refused to make any comment.

As for Miss Dora, the heroine of the scene which took place yesterday morning, callers are being told that she is indisposed.

The Mouse had spent the night at the Opera station where Lognon had not set foot. He had not hesitated to ask about the inspector, and the sergeant had made no attempt to conceal the truth.

'He went off yesterday on his annual leave . . . He'll

probably be leaving tomorrow or the day after for the Cantal, where he goes every year . . .'

The Mouse had spent the morning 'working' the churches: the Madeleine and Saint-Philippe-du-Roule. He had thought vaguely of going to the races in the afternoon, of taking *his* coach, and of making sure, without looking as if he were touching it, that the wallet was still behind the seat. But he had seen the midday paper at a kiosk and had changed his mind.

He could not have said what he had done until three o'clock in the afternoon. He had walked along the hot, empty street, and he had thought, or rather he had searched in vain for an inspiration.

He, who had never possessed anything, suddenly felt conscious of having a miser's soul. He was the rightful owner of that treasure deposited in Lost Property. It was his property, his possession, and the idea that it was in danger upset the old fellow so much that he started talking to himself as he dragged his leg along the pavements.

He even went so far as to utter astonishing remarks such as:

'There wouldn't be any justice left in this world . . .'

As time went by, he watched the police, to see whether they had been given any instruction about him yet.

For Lucile Boisvin could not fail to speak to the chief-inspector about his call and Lognon's.

He chuckled to himself at the thought that, if Lognon had not yet left, he would not be going on his holidays for some time. He nearly went up to the Place Constantin-Pecqueur, but it was too far, and at three o'clock he arrived at the Place Vendôme, prowled around the hotel for a quarter of an hour, and finally pushed the revolving door.

His first skirmish took place with the commissionaire, who tried to turn him out.

'I want to speak to the chief-inspector,' he declared. 'I've got something important to tell him . . .'

He said the same thing to the inspector who came to see what was happening, and who let him go up to the first floor, where the journalists were waiting in the lounge.

The Mouse was terribly scared. It was precisely for that reason that he embarked on his comic act once again before an audience all the more sympathetic in that his chatter provided them with picturesque copy.

'I ought to explain first of all that I live either in the Opera or the Grand Palais . . .' There was a roar of laughter straight away.

'In the basement, of course, I mean in the cells . . . Well, for years now I've had a pal who's what you might call my best enemy, Inspector Lognon, whom I nicknamed Inspector Grumpy . . . On Wednesday . . . No, on Thursday, in a bar in the Rue Washington – because I only move about in the best districts – I found a picture of a woman and I fell in love . . .'

He waved his arms about, with sweat streaming down his forehead, and at the same time he kept an eye on the door behind which Chief-Inspector Lucas and Lucile Boisvin were closeted.

It was then, at the height of the general hilarity, that that door had opened and they had heard the chief-inspector's: 'You seem to be forgetting, gentlemen, that there is *probably* a dead man in this case . . .'

Fountain-pens scribbled. The remark was written down word by word, and all the journalists underlined the word *probably* which, by itself, had frozen the smile on the Mouse's face.

What was happening now? The old man started trembling, trying to reassure himself by telling himself that the man was well and truly dead, that he couldn't have been mistaken to that extent.

His imagination started working. He wondered what would happen if, in a few minutes, when he in his turn was shown into the suite, he found himself face to face with the man in the car, alive and well, who would examine him, recognize him, and say: 'That's the man!'

'Go on, Mouse,' the reporters were saying. 'But don't talk so loud.'

He had lost the thread of his story, and passed his hand over his forehead.

'Where had I got to?'

'You were telling us about Inspector Grumpy . . .'

He made an effort to carry on where he had left off, but his heart was less and less in it, and he had all the trouble in the world to keep his eyes away from that door.

'You never wondered why your lover spent only two or three days with you every month?'

'He told me that he was travelling in the country . . .'

'And you were satisfied with that explanation?'

Chief-Inspector Lucas put his questions in a kindly way, always appearing to attach only minor importance to them. In the grey drawing-room, he was installed at a big Empire table, and from his seat he commanded a view of the Place Vendôme and the Rue de la Paix.

Lucile Boisvin, for her part, had sat down, at his invitation, on the very edge of an armchair. In this setting she looked more vulgar than in the flat in the Avenue du Parc-Montsouris. Her navy-blue dress looked skimpy. She adopted, in spite of herself, the humble attitude of a petitioner.

'I'm asking you whether that explanation satisfied you, whether you never had any suspicions.'

'No,' she said, shaking her head. 'I just thought that he had a wife somewhere else. He told me one day that

Protestants don't wear wedding rings ... All the same, I ought to have known that he wasn't what he said he was ...'

'Why?'

'I don't know ... wait a minute, though! I noticed that he didn't like going out with me and the boy except in popular places ... though I think that was a question of taste as well ... he always chose the local cinemas ... we often went to Luna Park, to the zoo, and to nearly all the exhibitions at the Porte de Versailles ...'

'And this struck you as peculiar?'

'Not that, no. I don't know how to explain. I didn't pay any attention at the time, but ever since this morning, little things have been coming back to me. How can I put it? He did all sorts of ordinary things with a pleasure that wasn't normal. Do you understand? Things like taking his jacket off when he arrived, putting on his slippers, and, in his shirt-sleeves, doing odd jobs like hammering nails in, putting a fresh washer in the tap, or mending the gramophone ... It was him that wanted us to eat in the kitchen, because he said it was cosier there ...'

Every now and then her eyelids puffed up and Lucas waited in silence. She sniffed, dabbed at her eyes, and went on:

'He was the finest man in the whole world. If he acted like that, I can understand it now, it was so as not to humiliate me, so as to come down to my level ... I often spoke to him about money ... I didn't want him to spend too much ... I used to say, for instance, that you travel just as fast second-class on the Métro as first ... Then he would look at me as if he found that rather touching ... That's something that ought to have intrigued me ...'

'How much did he give you a month?'

'There wasn't any fixed sum. I have an account book with each tradesman. When he came, he took all the account books. I can still see him in the dining-room in his shirt-sleeves, doing his accounts and putting the required sum of money on top of each book . . . With the rent, I didn't cost him as much as two thousand francs a month . . . I make my dresses and hats myself . . . Until last year, I made all the little boy's clothes too . . . When I think how I insisted on him opening an account with the Savings Bank!'

'Did he do that?'

'Yes . . . One day I even thought he was going to lose his temper . . . He used to put one hundred francs a month into the account . . . Well, on the sly, by cutting down a little on petty expenses, I managed to put a bit aside too, now and then . . . One morning, he checked the account . . . I thought he was going to fly into a temper. He smiled!'

She wasn't crying. She just had tears welling up under her eyelids, and a flush on her cheeks.

'Forgive my question, but was it passion which bound him to you?'

She understood straight away what he was insinuating. Her smile spoke volumes.

'Oh, you mustn't think that! He wasn't the dirty-minded sort . . .'

It was the chief-inspector's turn to smile, for that remark had suddenly betrayed the young woman's past.

'You know what I was when he met me. It was near the Gare Saint-Lazare, one evening about ten o'clock. I was sitting on the terrace of a brasserie and he was drinking beer at the next table. I spoke to him. I asked him if he would treat me to supper . . . Believe it or not, he didn't touch me for three weeks. First he wanted to get me away from the hotel and it was then that he fixed me up with that flat . . .'

'He never received any post there?'

She shook her head.

'No visitors either? He didn't talk to you about his friends or his family?'

'Only about his father, who died two years ago and

who he told me was a very strict Protestant . . . I think he was afraid of him . . .'

'You told me just now that you last saw him on Wednesday, at five o'clock in the afternoon, and that he was due to come back some time on Thursday.'

'Yes, that's what he told me. We'd been to Luna Park with the boy. He left us at the entrance to the Métro at the Porte Maillot . . .'

'He didn't say where he was going?'

'He never did.'

'And you never asked him?'

She shook her head.

'It's easy to see that you didn't know him! He wasn't the sort of man you asked questions. Besides, he'd have pretended not to hear.'

'How did he spend his evenings when he was at your place?'

'I've told you. He did odd jobs around the flat, or else he helped my son to sort out the stamps he brought for him.'

The chief-inspector stood up. He sensed that there was nothing more he could learn from her. Earlier on, when Lucile Boisvin had arrived, they had taken various items of clothing out of Loëm's wardrobe, which were still spread out on chairs. She had recognized two of them, two very quiet suits, one of which Leroy had worn at Luna Park on Wednesday, 23 June.

'You really think he's dead?' she asked now. 'It was when two people came and returned my photo that I had the feeling something was wrong . . .'

She had already told the chief-inspector about the two calls she had had on the Thursday and Friday, first from the Brown Man, as she called Lognon, then from the Old Man.

'Now I'd swear that there was only one copy of that photo in existence. Indeed I'd have liked to tear it up, because it

62

dated from the old days and it brought back unpleasant memories . . .'

'I'm going to ask you to give me a few minutes more,' said Lucas, making for the door, while at the noise all the journalists stood up together.

'It's the Inspector's fault . . .'

'Inspector Grumpy, I know.'

It was one of the worst quarters of an hour the Mouse had ever had. First of all, with his usual familiarity, he had made as if to sit down in one of the Empire armchairs, upholstered in green silk.

'On your feet!' was all that Lucas had said. Then, still putting on his act, the Mouse had picked up a paper-knife from the table, but the chief-inspector had taken it out of his hands.

'So it was on Thursday at three o'clock . . . You're sure it was three o'clock?'

'Yes . . . Or not far off . . . in the little bar in the Rue Washington . . . You must know it . . . The one where the liveried chauffeurs go for a quick drink . . .'

It was no use his sweating, gesticulating, trotting out all his jokes, performing his funniest mimes, he was constantly brought back to facts, dates, questions of time and place.

On Wednesday at such and such a time: the envelope . . .

On Thursday: the photograph . . .

On Thursday evening . . .

And so on. They were interrupted only by a telephone call and the chief-inspector went into the next room to take it, answering his caller:

'Tell him to come to the Hôtel Castiglione. Yes, I'll wait for him.'

And the old man went on:

'You understand, if I went along the Avenue du Parc-Montsouris, it was because I was intrigued. Why had the inspector pinched the photograph from me during the night? I had to give that photo back. That's all I know . . .'

For nearly another quarter of an hour, planted in front of one of the windows, Lucas let him go on talking by himself. Then at last he turned round, looking surprised to find the Mouse still there, and said:

'You can push off.'

'You don't want to know where to find me if you need me? You know, people sometimes hear about things . . .'

But the door was already open. And in the doorway there was a gloomy Lognon waiting. The chief-inspector scarcely gave the two men time to catch a glimpse of each other. He invited the inspector in while the Mouse posed once more for the photographers.

'He insisted that if I happened to learn anything . . . You understand? In our world it's rather like yours, gentlemen . . . By the way, did you see Inspector Grumpy?'

When Lognon came out, half an hour later, he did not see the Mouse as he had expected, and he never guessed that the old man, by means of his clowning, had managed to worm his way into the hotel kitchen, where the servants were splitting their sides over his story.

Lognon went home by the Métro. The dining-room was full of suitcases. His wife was standing at the window, with her hat on, and his son, dressed in his Sunday best, looked as if he did not know where to put himself.

'We're going to miss the train,' she said. 'How did it go?'

'We aren't going.'

Madame Lognon's shoulders drooped in vexation. She had spent twenty-four hours getting everything ready, buying things, and packing their bags to go and spend their holidays in the Cantal, only to be told at the last minute . . .

'Or else you could go alone with the boy. But I've got work to do in Paris . . .'

'Still because of that old man?'

'Him and some others . . . I can't tell you anything.'

For Lognon respected the seal of professional secrecy, and did not break it even in the privacy of his home.

'At least I hope it isn't dangerous . . .'

'Are you going or staying?'

'What do you think I should do?'

'Do as you like. I'm going back on duty at eight o'clock . . .'

Then she took her things off and undressed the boy, and the scene ended, while she was unpacking their luggage, in a fit of sobbing.

'I bet it's you again with your devotion to duty . . . I bet you asked to stay . . . Your wife doesn't count . . . Deny it if you dare . . .'

Deep in an easy chair, naked under a light dressing-gown, her chin resting on her hands, and a hard look in her eyes, Dora answered categorically:

'No!'

Chief-Inspector Lucas had had to ask to see her in her suite, for she had sent word to him that she was indisposed and that she did not want to come downstairs.

The rooms were in disorder. The bed, which he could see through the open door of the bedroom, still showed the hollow of a body, and all over the place there were pink cigarette ends, trays bearing half-empty glasses, a trolley carrying the remains of a cold lunch, and lastly, on a little table, a tube of aspirins.

'You are sure that you have never been on intimate terms with Monsieur Edgar Loëm . . .'

She shrugged her shoulders impatiently.

'Forgive me for pressing the point. Monsieur Müller

insinuates the contrary and mentions, in particular, a trip you went on recently to your country, to Budapest, with Loëm. Müller wasn't with you . . .'

'It was a business trip.'

'Can you tell me what sort of business was involved?'

'Am I forced to?'

'No. But our inquiries will tell us anything you keep back . . .'

'I went to Budapest to introduce Loëm to my father.'

'Why?'

'To pull off a big property deal which I don't know anything about myself . . . Loëm engaged in all sorts of business, such as aircraft firms and heavy industry, and he had even obtained the monopoly of the scent trade in some country or other in South America . . . Does that satisfy you?'

'Did the meeting between Loëm and your father lead to anything?'

Once again she replied in a fury:

'No!'

'Why not?'

'Because there wasn't any meeting.'

'But Loëm went to Budapest?'

'Yes.'

'And he didn't see your father?'

'He didn't see him because he'd changed his mind. Now are you satisfied?'

'One more question: How long have you been Müller's mistress?'

She stood up, very dignified, turned her back on the chief-inspector, and poured herself a drink, saying slowly and deliberately:

'I was his fiancée . . .'

Her attitude annoyed the chief-inspector so much that he couldn't resist the temptation to growl:

'Perhaps the two words mean the same thing in Hungarian? . . . But let's move on . . . How long was he your fiancé?'

'A year.'

'You lived on intimate terms with both men?'

'What does that mean? That I slept with them both?'

'I mean that you could go into both their suites, that they discussed their business in front of you . . .'

'No!'

'They kept it secret from you?'

'Loëm never discussed his business in front of anybody.'

'In that case, why did you accuse Frédéric Müller of killing his chief?'

'Because.'

'Because what?'

'Because he was capable of doing it.'

'Is that all?'

'Because he couldn't do anything else. Now I'd better tell you that I'm not going to say any more. It's finished. I'm tired. I'm ill. If you insist, I'll pick up the telephone and complain to my Minister . . .'

She had worked herself up to the same pitch of excitement as on the previous day, at the time of the scene in the lounge.

'I thought that the French had a certain reputation for gallantry . . .'

'I beg your pardon,' murmured Lucas rather unconvincingly. 'When you have decided to talk, will you ask for me at Police Headquarters, unless you prefer to speak straight away to the examining magistrate . . .'

'I've nothing more to say, seeing that you aren't prepared to arrest Müller . . .'

He bowed and went out, waiting for a moment, with his hand on the door handle, for a change of mind which didn't occur.

'Good night, Miss Dora . . .'

To which she replied in a fury:

'Go to hell!'

A reply which sounded pleasing only on account of her accent.

'You'll see tomorrow morning! I bet they'll put my photo on the front page . . .'

The Mouse had asked for a bed at the Opera station, and he had walked in like a film-star, for he knew that the whole station was familiar with his exploits. But in one corner he had caught sight of Lognon's gloomy face and he had cut his act short.

'Good night, Inspector Grumpy,' he had called out all the same as he went past.

He had been in bed for an hour now, and yet he could not manage to fall asleep, in spite of the two bottles to which he had treated himself at the end of the day. In front of him on the other side of the bars, he could see the legs, clad in light-coloured silk, of a prostitute who was sleeping sitting up, with her back against the wall and her head on one side.

Fortunately somebody was brought along to keep him company: a Pole whom he had already met and who began by being as sick as a dog.

'You don't know who I am? No? Well, old man, that's because you're a stranger to the district . . . I'm the Mouse . . . Monsieur Mouse, as the journalists call me . . . You'll see tomorrow . . . My photo on the front page of all the papers . . .'

The Pole was really ill and looked at him sourly. Possibly he didn't understand French very well either.

'The chief-inspector was a conceited character who thought he could do what he liked with me. "I beg your pardon," I said to him, "but I don't talk familiarly to people I don't know . . ."'

Usually he ended up by believing the stories he told like that. This time, Chief-Inspector Lucas was too much to swallow. And the Mouse finally lay down again, growling:

'Oh, you're too stupid to understand. You aren't worth the trouble of tiring myself out...'

They had set Lognon on him again, to swindle him out of his presbytery. But they had no idea yet what he was capable of. He didn't know himself, but he would think of something, and that very night too. Otherwise he was doomed to be a tramp all his life.

'Move your head, you mug, so that I can stretch my legs out.'

And just as he sank, earlier than he thought, into sleep, a word came back to him, like an air-bubble floating to the surface:

Archibald . . .

What the hell was Archibald doing in this business?

Chapter Five
Monsieur Martin Oosting
of Basle

It was Monday, 28 June. The schools had had to be given a day's holiday on account of the heat. Right in the centre of Paris, men could be seen walking about with their shirts open at the neck, and their jackets over one arm. The café terraces were lengthened and widened, and they buzzed with that excitement peculiar to exceptional days.

Not for anything in the world would Lognon have taken off his collar, even though it was a stiff collar with rounded cuffs to match. He was wearing his brown suit and brown hat as usual, and he had provided himself with a couple of handkerchiefs to mop his face.

Paris, that day, was not in the mood to take things seriously, and everybody had turned round to stare at a woman who had gone for a walk in beach pyjamas, and whom the newspaper photographers had not failed to notice.

In the offices work had slowed down, and in the streets the police were bringing a suitable indolence to the enforcement of the traffic regulations.

Lognon, for his part, remained as solemn as ever; it was in vain that the Mouse had tried for two hours to make him smile.

Had Chief-Inspector Lucas meant it literally when he had told the inspector:

'There may be something in it . . . Get on to the old fellow . . .'

The fact remained that Lognon was almost literally on top of him. He had spent the night at the Opera station.

Starting in the morning, he had followed the old man at a distance of less than three paces, and he had not batted an eyelid when the Mouse had stopped.

'Listen, Inspector . . . Don't you think we look silly following each other like this without saying a word? . . . If you like, we could walk together . . . It would be more fun that way too . . .' Lognon had simply turned his head the other way and remained standing in the middle of the pavement, as if nobody had spoken to him.

'All right . . . Just as you like . . . What I said was just as much for your sake as mine . . . They say that in the old days great lords always had a flunkey following them in the street . . .'

The Mouse was furious. He did not know where to go or what to do, and he tried to put the inspector off with the most unpredictable movements, suddenly starting to run, stopping in the same place for a quarter of an hour, setting off slowly and then darting into a shop.

Lognon kept on following him, all the gloomier in that he had just smoked his last cigarette and did not dare to abandon his pursuit to go into a tobacconist's.

Already, at ten o'clock in the morning, you could see men on the boulevards who had tucked handkerchieves under their hats to protect the backs of their necks.

At midday a paper came out with a few lines which looked quite insignificant:

THE DISAPPEARANCE OF THE SWISS FINANCIER

No headline this time. No captions. No photograph.

This morning, Monsieur Martin Oosting, Vice-President of the C.M.B., better known as the Basle Group, arrived in Paris by air, and booked in at a hotel in the Rue de Rivoli. He immediately had a number of conversations with, among others, the

Swiss Minister in Paris and a senior official of the Ministry of the Interior.

At eleven o'clock, Monsieur Oosting received Chief-Inspector Lucas at his hotel, and we understand that his report was of the greatest importance.

It seems, in fact, that an investigation was initiated too hurriedly, and undesirable publicity given to facts susceptible of a perfectly natural explanation.

According to Monsieur Martin Oosting, there is no reason to feel any anxiety over Monsieur Edgar Loëm's disappearance, for the latter, who liked peace and quiet, often retired for a few days to a country inn to rest.

In these circumstances it is quite possible that he has not read the reports of his disappearance which have been published in the newspapers these last few days.

Full stop. Nothing more about Müller, or about Miss Dora, or about Lucile Boisvin, or finally about the famous Mouse, whose photograph and hilarious statements were in all the morning papers.

Martin Oosting had tackled the matter at the top. He was a man with stubbly grey hair and black clothes hanging loosely over a fat, heavy body. From morning to night he smoked cigars without bothering whether the smoke blew into the faces of the people to whom he was talking.

If he had ever laughed, it must have been years before, during his childhood. When he entered a room, a sombre look in his eyes, crushing the floor beneath his heavy steps, it was impossible not to understand that he was the most important person present.

At the Hôtel du Louvre, everybody had realized that straight away, as soon as he got out of his taxi, when, without a word, with a categorical and almost threatening gesture, he had prevented the commissionaire from taking the little suitcase he was holding.

He had made for the reception desk and, looking down

at the young man in tails behind it, he had growled: 'Martin Oosting.'

For, of course, he had had a suite reserved for him. There was already a whole pile of telegrams waiting for him. Still standing, he ripped them open with one fingernail, and read them as if his gaze had been capable of crushing the letters on the paper.

He had not been there ten minutes before a car bearing a Diplomatic Corps plate drew up outside the hotel, and took him to see his Minister.

The latter, in his presence, and almost at his dictation, telephoned to the Ministry of the Interior, and accompanied the financier to the Place Beauvau.

There the telephone worked more than ever. The Prefect of Police was rung up and telephoned in his turn to the Director of Police Headquarters. From the Parquet, the call was transferred to the examining magistrate's chambers while Martin Oosting, thick and bulky, filled an armchair and smoked his cigar.

By eleven o'clock in the morning it was all over. It had been necessary to bow to the facts. Martin Oosting had convicted the French authorities of thoughtlessness and they had exculpated themselves by putting the blame for the whole unpleasant business on Chief-Inspector Lucas.

Oosting, who no longer had any need of his Minister, none the less kept the official car to take him back to the hotel. He received Lucas, in a room usually reserved for board meetings where there were twelve inkpots and twelve blotting-pads arranged on a baize table cover.

'You are the person who has come to record my official statement, are you? Take this down . . .'

He motioned to the chief-inspector to sit down in front of one of the blotting-pads. He for his part walked up and down, making the chandelier in the room below tremble, and stopping now and then to look over the police officer's shoulder.

. . . that nothing, either in the character of Monsieur Edgar Loëm, President of the C.M.B., or in his previous conduct, or in the state of his finance, gives reason to suppose that he may have been involved in any sort of untoward incident . . .

. . . that the anxiety shown by his employee Frédéric Müller is groundless . . .

He repeated the word *employee* twice, stressing each syllable.

. . . that it is regrettable that it should have been thought fit to give indecent publicity to certain details of his private life which have not even been proved . . .

Behind these words could be discerned the huge old-fashioned edifice of the C.M.B., in which for the past two centuries men as massive as Oosting or the carved furniture had gathered together in the council chamber, paved with black and white marble, and quietly, in an almost cathedral-like whisper, had organized colossal schemes.

'I shall be staying in Paris for a few days. It has been agreed with the Ministry that if you should learn anything, from whatever quarter, you should inform me immediately. That is all.'

At half past eleven, Lucas entered the office of the Director of Police Headquarters. At midday the latter was received by the Prefect. Finally at two o'clock the case was officially dropped, as a communiqué announced to the Press. However, the instructions given to Chief-Inspector Lucas were:

'Carry on quietly with the case.'

As for Lognon, who moved far below these inaccessible spheres, he went on stubbornly and heroically following the

Mouse, who was soon utterly worn out and ended up by dropping on to a bench in the Tuileries.

Martin Oosting, still on his feet, with his hands in the pockets of his baggy trousers, stood head and shoulders above Müller.

The two men had shut themselves up in Loëm's suite and Martin Oosting ostentatiously placed on a table a file bearing Müller's name.

'I'm listening.'

He was listening or he wasn't. It was impossible to tell. Smoking his cigar, he would go and plant himself in front of the window. Then he would come back to the Empire table and consult one of the papers in the file.

'On Wednesday the twenty-third of June,' Müller recited in a monotonous voice, 'Monsieur Loëm was away all afternoon. He came back about six o'clock and received two telephone calls which, contrary to his usual practice, he decided to answer himself. It was I who put these calls through to his bedroom, for he was dressing to go out.'

'What did you hear?' asked Oosting.

And, as he spoke, he opened the door of the adjoining office and lifted the receiver, to make sure Müller could have listened to the conversation.

The agent did not take offence. He accepted Oosting's supposition.

'The first time, a Monsieur John simply announced that the meeting would take place in Box 16 at the Opera.'

That explained the financier's white tie and tails, since it had been a gala performance.

'The second telephone call, at ten to eight, came from the same person . . .'

'This man John?'

'Yes . . . He said that he could not go to the Opera, but

75

that he would wait for Monsieur Loëm at the corner of the Rue de Berry . . .'

'At what time?'

'I assumed that it would be at nine o'clock, like the appointment at the Opera . . .'

Seeing Oosting toying with his watch chain, nobody could have guessed what he was thinking. Perhaps he believed all that he was being told, but perhaps he didn't believe a word of it.

'And then?'

'As I was in the lounge when Monsieur Loëm went out, he offered to drop me at the Madeleine.'

'And you weren't tempted to go and have a look at the corner of the Rue de Berry?'

'No.'

'Yes!'

'Yes . . . But I must have got there too late . . . I didn't see anybody . . .'

Still standing, Martin Oosting pretended to read a few of the documents in the file. They revealed that Müller, born into a lower middle-class family in Freiburg, had obtained his degree in law in that town and had then joined the legal department of the C.M.B.

For five years there was nothing but commonplace notes, regular salary increases, and reports by his departmental heads.

Then, all of a sudden, Edgar Loëm had taken him to Paris to negotiate a business deal, and had kept him there, first as his private secretary, then with the title of agent for the Group's French affairs.

Oosting made no comment. Chewing on his cigar, he examined from head to foot the elegant young man with the pomaded hair and the quiet tie, and it was as if these simple reports had a hidden meaning for him, as if they were enough to enable him to reconstruct a whole tragedy.

'When did you discover the existence of that woman?'

'Miss Dora?'

'No, the other one. Was it *before* or *after*?'

Müller must have understood, for he hurriedly answered: 'After.'

It was easy to see that he was lying, that he no longer had his former self-assurance.

'And Miss Dora?'

'She is my fiancée . . .'

'I hope that she has already left Paris.'

'She promised me that she would leave this evening . . . I thought it might be best for me to accompany her.'

'No!' snapped Oosting, slamming the file shut. 'Have you a typist?'

'She's in my office.'

'Send her to me . . . Then leave us alone.'

He dictated a whole series of coded telegrams. Then he asked for Brussels and Amsterdam on the telephone. At six o'clock in the evening, the drawing-room was blue with smoke, and in spite of all his cigars Martin Oosting had not even drunk a glass of water.

Inspector Joly, of Police Headquarters, discreetly informed Chief-Inspector Lucas that Miss Dora, whom Müller had accompanied to the Gare du Nord, had just got on the Berlin express with a ticket for that city.

'Let her go,' Lucas replied over the telephone. 'Follow Müller . . .'

As for Inspector Grumpy, he was getting farther and farther from the centre of affairs. The Mouse, possibly in a spirit of vengeance, had led him all the way along the banks of the Seine to Charenton Lock.

As the hours had gone by, the sky had become heavier, the atmosphere stormier. Lognon wondered how the old tramp, with his limping gait, could cover mile after mile like that. The two of them had lunched in a Bargees' café on the Quai de Bercy. The Mouse, who had a few francs in his pocket, had confined himself, as usual, to some bread, sausage and red wine. At three o'clock in the afternoon he arrived at the lock which enables boats to cross from the Seine to the Marne, and there, among five hundred people who were doing the same, lay down on the sparse grass of the canal bank, put his jacket rolled up into a ball under his head, his bowler hat over his face, and apparently went to sleep.

Lognon nearly took the opportunity to rush to the nearest bar and telephone to Chief-Inspector Lucas, under whose orders he considered himself to be for the time being. But he was afraid that the Mouse's sleep might be just a ruse, and he remained sitting on the grass, on which he had spread his handkerchief so as not to dirty his trousers.

Some boys were bathing. A few of them, the smallest, were completely naked, and if the inspector had been in his own sector he would have forced them to get dressed. Fifty barges were waiting while others squeezed into the lock, which seemed too narrow for their huge bellies.

About five o'clock, the old man moved. His hat slipped off his face, and, laboriously raising himself, the Mouse looked around him, saw that he was now right out in the sun and dragged himself two yards farther on, giving a sour look at Lognon.

This joke no longer amused him. It was he who had grown tired of it first and who was beginning to feel frightened. So it was only half-heartedly that he poked his tongue out, a gesture which failed to provoke the slightest quiver in the inspector's face.

First of all he decided to go and have a drink, although he already had a headache from sleeping out in the sun. He drank some red wine as usual, while his shadow remained planted on the kerb. A newspaper was lying on the bar counter and he asked:

'Can I take it?'

'If you like . . .'

'I'll take the rest of the bottle too . . .' he announced. 'That's how much?'

He went back to the grassy bank by the canal, where at six o'clock, when work stopped in the factories and offices, there was, so to speak, not a single place left. Swimmers were diving from the barges, sending sheaves of water into the air.

The old man read the paper without looking at the date. He read everything which fell under his eyes, a story of a tax fraud, an article on tuberculosis in childhood, and scores of advertisements, including one which interested him, for it recommended a truss and he happened to suffer from a hernia.

Now and then he took a swig of wine and darted a glance at Lognon, who, without appearing to do so, was ogling a rather buxom girl who was bathing, and one of whose shoulder-straps was showing a tendency to slip.

Second-hand car for sale . . .
Earn six hundred francs a month in your spare time . . .

And then, all of a sudden, among the classified advertisements, three lines leaped to the Mouse's eye.

Archibald. Profit. arrang. Any day 8 p.m. Fouquet's holding *New York Herald* Discr. guarant.

At first he frowned, making an effort to try to understand the abbreviations. He ended up by translating the advertisement as follows:

Archibald. Profitable arrangement. Present yourself any day at eight o'clock in the evening opposite Fouquet's, holding a copy of the *New York Herald*. Discretion guaranteed.

He darted yet another glance at Lognon, who was taking no notice of him, put the newspaper on the grass and started thinking.

He could be mistaken, of course. The fact remained that he could have sworn that the Archibald in question was himself. Straight away he felt a prickling in his legs, was filled with an urge to walk and wave his arms about, and kept looking at Lognon with the secret intention of giving him the slip at the slightest opportunity.

Had he been mistaken when he had thought that there was a man in the car, behind the corpse? Whether he had been in the car or somewhere else did not matter. What mattered was that somebody had seen him opening the car door and probably picking up the wallet too.

The murderer or murderers. And they were afraid of him. Perhaps they wanted to get the dollars back?

In any case, they were using the classified advertisements to get in touch with him. How could they attract his attention without attracting that of the police?

By means of Archibald, of course. The name which was written on the envelope and which was not particularly common.

The Mouse stood up, asked one of his neighbours what time it was, and when he learnt that it was already half past six, hurried towards the tram stop. This time it was with anger, even fury, that he looked at Lognon, who stood waiting beside him. Not to mention the fact that a thought occurred to him which complicated everything.

How did the murderer or murderers, who had not been in possession of the wallet, know the name Archibald?

Was he to assume that they knew that that envelope was in the dead man's pocket?

And to think that the Mouse, who had had it in his hands, had not examined it! It had struck him as of no importance. An old envelope with nothing in it, that was all. And now it was impossible to go and look for it in the coach without that fellow Lognon . . .

They were both on the platform of the tram, travelling back to Paris along the quays.

'Listen, Monsieur Lognon . . .'

The other man looked at him without batting an eyelid.

'Don't you think we look a bit silly, the two of us? Not to mention the fact that you didn't have much of a lunch! You'll have an even worse dinner if I take it into my head to roam around some waste land until it's dark . . .'

Silence on Lognon's part.

'What would you say if I proposed an armistice? I'll let you go and have your dinner in peace with Madame Lognon and meet you at, say, nine o'clock, outside the Opera station . . .'

He nearly stamped his foot with rage. Lognon did not answer him. Lognon looked at him with a gaze as vacant as if the tramp had been transparent and the inspector had been unable to see anything through him but the macadam gliding along beside the tram.

'Well, never mind,' muttered the Mouse.

He got off at the Louvre, seeing that the tram did not go any farther. It was ten past seven. He told himself that he would try to shake off the inspector on the Métro, and he was making for the station when Lognon passed him and jumped on to the platform of a moving bus.

'Well, I'll be damned!'

Five minutes earlier, he had been cursing the presence of Inspector Grumpy, and now he was grumbling about this inexplicable flight.

What could have happened to induce him to go off like that?

Every window in Paris was open. The evening was as stifling as the day had been, but there were grounds for hoping that a storm might break during the night. In the

Rue de Rivoli, the Mouse stopped at a newspaper kiosk and, after hesitating for a moment, asked:

'Have you got any papers left from yesterday or the day before yesterday?'

'I'll see . . .'

The newspaper vendor found two. He opened them at the classified advertisements page and found the three lines addressed to Archibald. Perhaps – who could tell? – the advertisement had started to appear as early as the previous Thursday, the day after Monsieur Loëm's disappearance.

'Give me the *New York Herald*.'

This time the newspaper vendor looked at him with amazement, shrugged her shoulders, but held out the American paper all the same, a paper of thirty-six pages which the Mouse had all the trouble in the world to stuff into his pocket.

He was impatient now. Impatient and anxious. It seemed to him that it was the fate of his presbytery which was going to be decided, on the stroke of eight, in front of Fouquet's, on the Avenue des Champs-Élysées.

An ironic fate dictated that after the purchase of the *New York Herald* the Mouse should have only thirty centimes left, too little to enable him to use any means of transport whatever.

Passers-by turned round to look at this little old man who was hurrying alone, panting and sweating, and who seemed to be pursuing some mysterious objective.

'Archibald . . .'

To keep his spirits up, he kept repeating these three syllables, muttering menacingly:

'We'll see . . . If they think they can get the better of me . . .'

He chuckled to himself. He recalled Chief-Inspector Lucas who had treated him with cold contempt, Lognon who had imagined that he could do what he liked with him, and all the others, the journalists, the inspectors from

Police Headquarters, everybody who was looking for Monsieur Loëm's murderer . . .

While he, the Mouse, was coming to the Place de la Concorde, crossing the square between the moving taxis, and running up the Champs-Élysées. He, the Mouse, who at eight o'clock was going to find himself in the presence of the murderers.

He did not know yet what he was going to do. All the same, he took the precaution of making sure that the American paper did not poke out of his pocket. Like that, he would have time to see what was coming, to show himself openly when he wanted to, and probably not to show himself at all.

Ten to eight . . . He could see the time by the clock on the Eiffel Tower which was lit up although night had not yet fallen. Bluish shadows were nestling in the foliage of the trees. There were people everywhere, sweethearts sauntering along at random, and families with children being pulled along by the hand and smaller ones who had to be carried.

Five to eight . . .

An amusing thought made him laugh, in spite of his tiredness: what if the British Ambassador were there too, for it was his name in the advertisement?

Confidential. A telegram received from Budapest Police Headquarters in response to a request for information confirms that the barrister Staori, the father of Dora Staori, has for a long time been in a fairly precarious situation . . .

Lucas was working all alone in his office, from which he could see the Place Saint-Michel and the left bank of the Seine. He picked up the telephone and listened for a moment.

'That's correct,' he said. 'It's true that there is no reason to suppose that anything sinister has happened . . . Why, yes . . . It's best to look on the bright side of things . . . I promise . . .'

It was Lucile Boisvin, who, at the other end of the line, was asking him for news. She had read in the evening papers Oosting's statement that he refused to believe in either a crime or a suicide.

After hanging up the receiver, Lucas shrugged his shoulders, had a drink of beer, and went on:

. . . due to his way of life, Staori, in fact, who has a brilliant mind but possesses no personal fortune, leads a life of luxury and gives lavish receptions every winter. Three years ago he was nearly involved in a financial scandal. Harried by his creditors, he has only managed to carry on these last few months thanks to the confidence inspired by the Basle Group, to which his future son-in-law Frédéric Müller belongs.

Has organized a big property enterprise in which the Group is due to invest considerable capital.

Underneath, Lucas wrote in a smaller hand:

Note: it seems that Müller, on making the acquaintance of Dora Staori, probably in the course of a trip to Budapest, boasted of his post in the C.M.B. It also seems that he persuaded Monsieur Loëm to travel to Budapest to examine this new enterprise. But it appears that the Swiss financier, although accompanied by the girl, received unfavourable information about Staori as soon as he arrived in the Hungarian capital, for he refused to see him.

It should be noted that Monsieur Martin Oosting treats Müller as a minor employee, whereas Monsieur Loëm often seemed to submit to his influence.

I am trying, with the discretion called for in the circumstances, to find out whether the influence Müller exerted on Loëm was not due to the fact that Müller knew about his chief's liaison with a former prostitute, by whom, what is more, he had a son.

The mentality of the people in the Basle Group, illustrated by the personality of Martin Oosting, makes this theory plausible, and this would explain a good many things . . .

At this point, Chief-Inspector Lucas, who had not interrogated the Mouse as closely as he might have done, went off the rails, for he added:

... including the possible flight of a Loëm driven to breaking-point by blackmail.

This was not an official report but just a minute destined for the Prefect of Police, who would do what he liked with it.

After this, Lucas finished his beer, wiped his mouth, picked up his hat and took a bus home.

The smarter the social class in Paris, the later it dines, and when the Mouse reached Fouquet's on the corner of the Champs-Élysées and the Avenue George V, there were still two hundred people on the terrace, a good many of whom were carrying field-glasses which had been used in the afternoon at Maisons-Laffitte.

The old tramp, who was finding it difficult to get his breath back, was slightly taken aback by this crowd, and he decided to scout around before taking the *New York Herald* out of his pocket.

'Excuse me, ladies and gents ... You wouldn't have a couple of francs to spare for me to go and drink a beer to your health?'

This was the best means, indeed the only means at his disposal, of getting a close look at all the customers, especially as there was no uniform in sight.

He limped about. He threaded his way between the tables, avoiding the waiters – who were worse than the police in this sort of establishment – and had some difficulty in smiling on account of his rapid breathing.

'My respects, Your Highness ... I bet you've got too much change in your pocket ... There's nothing worse for spoiling the shape of clothes ...'

All his old tricks, in fact. Making people laugh instead of rousing their pity . . .

'If I'd known you were going to Maisons-Laffitte, I'd have given you the winner of the third race, seeing that the jockey and I are twins . . .'

There were six rows of tables, not counting those on the other side, in the Avenue George V. A lot of women. A few tables with only men sitting at them, but nobody who made the Mouse think of Archibald. He spoke to some Germans in German and picked up two francs at one go.

He was approaching the corner when all of a sudden he saw something which made him wish he could sink into the ground: Lognon was there – yes, Inspector Grumpy with his brown suit, his round cuffs, his stiff collar.

But a Lognon who had not even seen the Mouse, he seemed to be so absorbed in his perusal of the *New York Herald*.

So he had come here too in answer to the advertisement! Unless . . .

No. He was not intelligent enough to have put it in the papers. The proof of that was that when he saw the tramp, he tried to hide behind his paper and, failing to do so, called the waiter and paid for his drink.

It was ten past eight. Nobody had spoken to Lognon, in spite of the ostentatious way in which he had brandished the American paper.

The Mouse caught up with him ten yards from the terrace, and allowed himself the malicious pleasure of saying teasingly:

'I didn't know you could read English.'

'And what were you doing there?'

'My business, as you could see for yourself . . . Eleven francs fifty in a few minutes . . .'

He showed a handful of small change, but took care not to display the newspaper which was filling his pocket.

Chapter Six
Inspector Lognon's
Two Blunders

Lognon was not only in a bad temper but annoyed with himself. That morning his wife had told him once again:

'It's your own fault. Why must you always push yourself forward? . . . Especially seeing that you've always gone when it's time to pick the chestnuts out of the fire . . .'

It was midnight and only now was he making his way home, never guessing that that very evening he had just perpetrated two blunders, one of which he was going to pay for straight away.

The first blunder had been failing to search the Mouse. For several days the old tramp had been unable to set foot in a police station without being searched from head to foot, and that at Lognon's request.

Now, the inspector had just spent a disappointing day, glued, so to speak, to the tramp. He had let go of him for an hour, just long enough to go to Fouquet's as he had already done the day before, in an attempt to discover the person or persons responsible for the advertisement.

He had found the Mouse again, and, almost by accident, on the terrace of that establishment, he had thought of everything except searching him.

It had not even been forgetfulness. Lognon had been dazed by the heat and by weariness and boredom. His obsession had begun to go stale on him, and he had nearly let the Mouse go off wherever he liked.

This time it had been the old man who had hung on to him.

'I'm going to put a proposal to you . . . As you obviously can't bear to leave me, why don't we plan our time together? . . . Look here, I feel like treating myself to the flicks . . . After that, well, you can take me to the Opera station, and your mind will be at rest . . .'

Lognon had accepted. For nearly three hours, in the cinema, he had brushed against the Mouse's pocket, and, in that pocket, the *New York Herald*.

If he had found it, he would have realized that the old man had kept the appointment and then he would probably have deduced that . . .

The other blunder was more recent. At the Opera station, where he had accompanied the Mouse, Lognon had handed him over to a young colleague, adding, not without a certain pride:

'On the orders of Chief-Inspector Lucas of Police Headquarters. Special mission . . .'

Then he had jumped on the bus which stops at the Place Clichy. There, to reach home, he could have taken a second bus, but as this had been a long time coming, he had decided to go up the Rue Caulaincourt on foot.

He scarcely realized what happened next. He was less than a quarter of a mile from the red light of a police station. He was wondering why, in spite of the *New York Herald*, the person responsible for the advertisement had twice failed to appear.

A car passed him and drew up a few yards ahead. A man got out, made as if to cross the pavement and collided with the inspector as if by accident. Instead of apologizing, and as Lognon was bending down to pick up his hat, the stranger hit him hard on the head, probably with a small rubber truncheon, for the inspector lost consciousness.

It was the police motor-cyclists who found him a few minutes later and who telephoned the emergency service, with the result that Lognon had the honour of bringing out the Eighteenth Arrondissement police van, and if he had not come to on the way, he would have recovered consciousness in a hospital bed.

'It's nothing,' he murmured. 'Take me home . . .'

He had a terrible headache, but no bones broken. He was helped into the lift, which suddenly made him feel sick, and taken up to the fourth floor.

Madame Lognon awoke.

'Is that you, Joseph?'

'Yes,' he growled.

He insisted on offering a drink to the two policemen, who had helped him. Madame Lognon lost patience. She came into the dining-room in her nightdress, with her hair in curlers, and could not manage to understand why her husband, at such a time of night, should be taking out of the sideboard the carafe of calvados and the best glasses with the gilt edges.

She understood even less why, when he was filling the glasses, he suddenly staggered, just had time to sit down on a chair, and fainted.

'I've always told him so,' she declared when the policemen had told her about the attack. 'Now he's a lot better off!'

So much better off that the doctor had to be sent for in the middle of the night, for Lognon had a raging fever. As there was only one bedroom for the whole family of three, the boy could not sleep, and in the morning his mother decided to keep him at home.

The local chief-inspector came in person about ten o'clock to see the wounded man, who would need a good week to get back on his feet, and the best glasses were brought out again.

As for the Mouse, he wondered why, once again, Inspector Grumpy was leaving him to his own devices, or rather why he was entrusting him to the care of a young inspector whom he could have shaken off within a few minutes if he had wanted to.

That same morning, the plane from Basle brought a personage to Le Bourget who was similar in every respect to the one it had brought the day before, in other words Monsieur Oosting.

The new arrival was called Gade, and his hair, instead of being grey, was red. But he smoked the same cigars, and looked at people with the same calm, utterly contemptuous eyes.

Monsieur Gade, managing director of the C.M.B., did not entrust his pigskin briefcase stuffed with papers to any porter. He gave a taxi-driver the address of the Hôtel du Louvre where, in the morning, before he had arrived, he had already been asked for twice on the telephone, from Switzerland and Belgium.

'Send the barber up to me,' he said as he entered the lift. He had a thick red skin, with a coarse texture, like that of certain oranges. His stubbly hair had a sort of sunset glow. When he was ready, he telephoned to Monsieur Oosting, whose suite was on the same floor, and the two men shut themselves up in a drawing-room, each bringing along his own briefcase, while the telephone rang again and again, now for one, now for the other.

Chief-Inspector Lucas, during the war, had served in Military Intelligence, and had been entrusted with various missions in Switzerland. He had kept some friends in the Swiss police and it was to one of these that he telephoned.

Unlike Lognon, he refused to allow this case to hypnotize him. He was extremely preoccupied, among other things, by the discovery of a murdered boy in the Paris suburbs, a discovery which had once again brought a horde of press-men to the door of his office.

If he continued to take an interest in Loëm, it was because orders from above had said:

'Carry on quietly with your inquiries.'

This meant compiling a file, just in case, so as to be prepared if there were a sudden development. For example, if the financier's body were found.

After his telephone call to Switzerland, he wrote a note which went to join other notes in the manila folder:

The Loëm family has been at the head of the C.M.B. or Basle Group for three generations. In Switzerland people often call it, without the slightest irony, the Loëm dynasty.

Grandfather Loëm was an impressive figure: a liberal economist and an uncompromising puritan.

His son, the father of the present Loëm, copied his facial expressions and his gait, going so far as to wear, at the beginning of the twentieth century, clothes more or less identical to those which the old man wore forty years before.

Edgar Loëm was not really due to succeed his father, for he had an elder brother who was destined for that task, but who died in a mountaineering accident.

Edgar Loëm is not regarded as a financial genius: he carries on the family tradition, that is all, surrounded by eleven gentlemen whose families, like his, have belonged to the Basle Group for several generations.

In Switzerland he is not known to have any liaison. It was rumoured for a while that he was going to marry his brother's widow, but nothing of the sort has happened.

During this time the two gentlemen from Basle had left the Hôtel du Louvre and walked over to the neighbouring Hôtel Castiglione, where they went into Loëm's suite.

The communicating door leading into Müller's office was open. Müller was there, working. He stood up stiffening to greet the two men who did not seem to notice his presence, and whose combined cigars had soon turned the air blue.

Calmly and methodically, as was only to be expected, the two men opened first the safe and then the drawers, heaped the files on the desk and examined them one by one, occasionally taking notes, and now and then showing each other an important document without needing to exchange any words.

As they were looking for the key to a small piece of furniture in Loëm's drawing-room, Müller held it out to them, saying:

'All it contains is the stamp collection . . .'

There were two albums, plus a number of transparent paper envelopes, each of which contained a single stamp.

While Oosting did not drink at all, Gade drank whole goblets of iced tea and sweated equivalent amounts through all the pores of his granulous skin.

At noon, the two men did not trouble to go to lunch, but ordered sandwiches which they ate while they worked.

They did not know that the Budapest–Prague–Paris plane had brought along, at ten past nine, a new character, and that Chief-Inspector Lucas was once again at grips with the Diplomatic Corps.

For Francis Staori, an extremely good-looking man with a matt complexion, whose rather insipid perfume had impregnated the plane, set about things in exactly the same way as these gentlemen of the financial world.

At ten o'clock he was seeing his Minister. At half past ten, in the latter's company, he entered the Ministry of the Interior where an official greeted him with marked politeness.

The only difference was that Staori talked, and talked volubly, with an accent no less attractive than his daughter's. He made a vehement protest against the French police who had brought disgrace upon his family by making public personal details which in any case he declared to be false.

Dora had never been Müller's mistress. Only somebody with the French mentality, which saw sex in everything, could consider it strange for a girl to spend a year in Paris in the same hotel as her fiancé.

Staori refused to commit himself as to the consequences which might result from such publicity, and demanded an immediate correction in the newspapers.

The storm had still not broken, and in the course of all these conversations, damp hands were shaken, the same gesture of face-mopping was made, and through the wide-open windows the clatter of typewriters could be heard.

The official promised, of course, to do everything in his power. Then, as he had done the day before, he telephoned to the Prefect of Police, who telephoned to the Director of Police Headquarters, who summoned Lucas to his office.

'There you are! He arrived in Paris this morning. He's staying at the Hôtel Castiglione in his daughter's suite. He absolutely insists on dictating a statement to the Press and he's asking for a press conference to be called this afternoon ...'

The two men looked at each other with the same grimace. They could not prevent Staori from telling the journalists anything he liked. But then the others, the men from Basle, would once again bring their Minister along to the Place Beauvau to make a fresh protest.

'What do you think about it all, Lucas?'

Lucas answered unsmilingly:

'I'd like to see the corpse!'

'If there is a corpse.'

'And I'd like to find that car ...'

Its number and description had been circulated to all the police forces in France, at the same time as the description of the ten or twelve cars stolen in Paris every day. Only both men belonged to Police Headquarters, and they were well aware that out of those twelve cars fewer than half were recovered. If that. And often several months later.

'What do you intend to do?'

'I'm going to see this fellow Staori . . .' At that moment the telephone rang and, as Lucas made as if to leave, the Director of Police Headquarters, who had picked up the receiver, motioned to him to take the second earphone.

'Hullo . . . Yes . . . Will you say that again?'

'This is the local chief-inspector of the Ninth Arrondissement. Inspector Lognon was attacked last night in the Rue Caulaincourt by somebody who got out of a car . . . He was hit on the head with a blunt instrument and is now confined to bed at his home at the Place Constantin-Pecqueur . . . It's he who has just asked me to notify Police Headquarters, and in particular Chief-Inspector Lucas . . . Is he there?'

'He's here with me. Thank you very much.'

'Will you ask him if he wants us to keep on shadowing the Mouse? I'm short of men, and if it wasn't necessary any more . . .'

The Director looked questioningly at Lucas, who shrugged his shoulders.

'All right. In that case drop it . . .'

When he had hung up, the Director asked:

'What's all this about the Mouse?'

'An idea of Inspector Lognon's . . . It's a fact that the old man seems to know something . . . But what? . . . I'll question him tonight . . .'

They remained silent for a moment. Then Lucas murmured:

'I bet Müller didn't leave the Hôtel Castiglione last night . . . As for Staori, if what we've heard is true, he wasn't in France at the time . . .'

He repeated in conclusion:

'What do you expect? I'd give a great deal to see the corpse . . .'

The Director could have been mistaken. But he had the impression that the chief-inspector did not believe very fervently in the existence of that corpse.

Before going up to the third floor of the hotel, Lucas sent his card up to the gentlemen from Basle, asking them for a moment's conversation. They replied through the third floor waiter that they were extremely busy and asked the chief-inspector to come back in the evening or to write to them.

These people were obviously anything but overawed by the police. They went on working in the office, which smelled of cigars and Müller's brilliantine.

Then Lucas wrote on a piece of paper:

Can you tell me whether the C.M.B. was officially planning to bring off a real estate deal in Budapest, through the medium of or with the collaboration of the barrister Staori?

He sent up this note, which was returned to him bearing the one word in red pencil:

'No!'

Lucas nearly took the lift. He changed his mind, turned the scrap of paper over, and this time wrote:

Was Monsieur Edgar Loëm free to open negotiations for a deal of this sort without consulting the board of directors?

The same note came back with the same word written in the same hand:

'No!'

Then the chief-inspector heaved a sigh of satisfaction and had his name sent in to Staori. He found him in the company of a Hungarian friend of his who lived in Paris and whom Lucas had the impression of having seen some-where.

To begin with, Staori got on his high horse, repeated what he had said in the morning, spoke of his family's honour, of the Budapest bar, of the whole of his country in fact, which had been defiled by this affair.

'I want the journalists to come here, and I shall tell them . . .'

Lucas listened patiently. He was hot, too, but he did not take the trouble to mop his streaming forehead. While the other was talking, he toyed with the piece of paper, and suddenly he held it out to Staori, who glanced at it, faltered, and stammered:

'What is it?'

'Two little questions that I've just put in writing to those gentlemen of the Basle Group . . .'

'But . . . I don't see . . . How does this concern me?'

Then, slowly and clumsily, the chief-inspector felt in all his pockets before finally taking out the telegram from the Budapest police.

So much the worse for the Budapest police: Staori could tackle them if he wanted to.

. . . confirms that the barrister Staori, the father of Dora Staori, had for a long time been in a fairly precarious situation . . .

The barrister was now regretting the presence of his fellow countryman, whom a little earlier he had been so happy to call to witness.

. . . has only managed to carry on these last few months thanks to the confidence inspired by the Basle Group to which his future son-in-law . . .

During this time Lucas assumed an imbecilic expression, filled a pipe, hesitated to light it. He waited. He took back his telegram and his piece of paper.

'This is a plot by political enemies who want to ruin me!' Staori exclaimed in the end. 'And, incidentally, I'd very much like to know how this document came into your possession.'

'Through the most administrative of channels . . . You will notice that I haven't used it . . . It would be really deplorable if the Press . . .'

'They haven't any right . . .'

'That was just what I was going to say . . . if the Press, who have got into the habit of carrying out certain inquiries themselves, and who are sometimes quite clever at it, should publish information of this sort which might come to them from other quarters . . . I can answer for the discretion of our services, but the same may not be true of Budapest . . . Remember that the whole case has been more or less dropped, seeing that no corpse has been found, and in the absence of any complaint the investigation has been called off . . . Monsieur Müller, who was really just a rather minor employee, has abused your trust and that of your daughter . . . The readers of the French press have already forgotten this story, and if we take care not to rake it up again . . .'

'Will you have something to drink, Chief-Inspector?'

'I wouldn't say no to a beer.'

And the whole thing finished as it was bound to, with Staori complaining of the perfidy of the gentlemen of the Basle group, who had abused his trust and were now going back on their word.

'For Monsieur Loëm did come to Budapest to see me! If we didn't meet, that was because I was involved in a case being tried in the provinces and he couldn't wait for me . . .'

An admirable beer was served, and a whisky for Staori, who accompanied the chief-inspector to the door.

'I suppose that documents of this sort . . .'

'Never leave my files. I may add that as soon as the case has been officially dropped, they will be destroyed.'

'I count on you,' said Staori with a meaning wink. 'In any case, we shall meet again . . .'

He went back into his suite, convinced that he had bought off Chief-Inspector Lucas.

As for the latter, he would have given a great deal to have even the smallest piece of information on this case, in which he could see all the traps, but in which, try as he might, he could not make out the tiniest clue.

The sun was beating down so hard that it seemed a positive expedition just to cross the Place Vendôme. At the door of the hotel, the chief-inspector hesitated for a moment, shrugged his shoulders at the sight of his inspector, who was pacing up and down the pavement with a fake discretion calculated to attract the attention of the least perceptive of onlookers, hailed a taxi, and, after a final hesitation, said half-heartedly.

'The Place Constantin-Pecqueur.'

The order to drop the shadowing of the old Mouse had not had time to reach the person concerned, as Lucas realized on seeing, a few yards from Lognon's home, a young man as unconvincingly casual as the first, to whom he spoke.

'M.P.?' he asked.

Municipal police? And the other, recognizing the chief-inspector, whose photograph appeared nearly every week in the papers, stammered:

'Yes . . . You know about it all?'

'So he's upstairs, is he?'

'He's just arrived. This morning, when he left the station, he went to the banks of the Seine, stripped to the waist, and cleaned himself up. With a crowd of amused spectators, he washed from head to foot, or nearly, and then he went and sat down on a bench in the shade. At midday bought the paper that had just come out, and it was then that he found out that the Inspector had been the victim of an attack. He must have hesitated about coming, because he took a round-about route to get here.'

Lucas asked the concierge which floor to go to, took the lift, rang the bell of the Inspector's flat, and greeted Madame Lognon, who, on hearing his rank, scowled instead of behaving more pleasantly.

'Come in,' was all that she said.

Then she muttered under her breath, as if talking to herself:

'If they think this is the way to treat a man with a temperature like that!'

There were only three rooms: the kitchen, the dining-room and the bedroom. The little boy, in the dining-room, did not know what to do. The bedroom door was closed.

'You want me to announce you?'

'If that isn't too much trouble.'

The next moment, the Mouse rushed out of the room, so fast that he nearly fell over a chair. Lognon could be seen sitting up in bed, with his head wrapped in a compress.

'Wait for me here,' Lucas said to the Mouse, before going into the bedroom and shutting the door behind him.

Then he said:

'Hullo, Inspector . . . So you stopped a real good 'un, did you?'

Lucas was embarrassed. Never, even when his little boy had made his first communion, had his humble home seen so many distinguished visitors. The local chief-inspector in the morning. Chief-Inspector Lucas in the afternoon . . . He glanced anxiously around to make sure that everything was tidy, and called out to his wife:

'Bring the armchair for the chief-inspector . . .'

For there was only one in the whole flat, on account of the lack of space.

'You know, I'd have got up, if it had been left to me . . . It's the doctor who says . . .'

'Don't you worry, old chap . . . I just dropped in to say hullo . . . You were out of luck last night, because, knowing you as I do, if they hadn't set about it so cunningly . . .'

'Like professionals,' exclaimed Lognon, bursting with pride. 'I didn't have time to see a thing. If I was brought face to face with my attacker tomorrow, I wouldn't recognize him . . . I didn't see anything, either the colour of the car or its number . . . But there's at least one thing I've tumbled to, and that's their trick . . .'

'Ah?'

What luck, Lucas seemed to be thinking, that at last somebody understands something.

Lognon explained to him the business of the advertisement, which he had read as far back as Sunday and which had led him to go to Fouquet's with the *New York Herald*.

'You understand? They had to find out whether anybody was in the know . . . They put the advertisement in the papers . . . But instead of showing themselves, they stood in a corner to watch . . . They spotted me, thanks to the American paper . . . They said to themselves that I knew something . . .'

'Whereas, in fact, you don't know anything,' said Lucas calmly.

Lognon gave a start, thought for a moment, and conceded:

'Yes, it's true, I don't know anything!'

'In that case,' the chief-inspector went on, 'I wonder who does know something. For they didn't insert that advertisement just to arouse our curiosity . . . They are worried about somebody . . .'

'I can see that you've got the same idea as me . . .'

He thought that perhaps he had gone too far, that the chief-inspector might be annoyed, and he hurriedly added:

'I beg your pardon . . .'

'Not at all! Not at all! You've shown considerable initiative . . .'

Suddenly changing tone, he asked:

'What's the old man doing here?'

He had put Lognon so completely at his ease that the inspector answered normally, as he would have spoken to his wife, and not as he was accustomed to address his superiors.

'I was wondering about that too . . . If I told you what I really think . . .'

'Go on . . . Tell me . . .'

'It's rather silly . . . I've never been at all gentle with him . . . Well, when he came along tonight, I got the impression that it was practically a friendly call . . . He seemed embarrassed about what had happened to me . . . He said he hoped that I wasn't in any pain . . .'

Lognon was afraid of appearing the sentimental sort. Consequently he corrected himself:

'I know perfectly well that he's a play-actor . . . But in that case, why should he have come?'

Through the open window they could see children playing in the square, and they could hear a shrill noise like the sound of a school playground.

'I don't know if you understand what I mean . . .'

And he reddened, fearing once again that he had annoyed the chief-inspector.

'It's difficult to explain . . . The very first evening, when I saw the Mouse bring in the envelope with the dollars, I sensed that there was something wrong . . .'

'Incidentally,' Lucas broke in, 'where is that envelope?'

'It must be in Lost Property . . . You're right, though!'

He guessed what his chief was thinking. Nobody had

thought yet of examining the famous envelope, or of publishing the numbers of the notes.

'I can see what you're going to do . . .'

Damn! He had gone too far. Lucas could not like somebody else to guess his thoughts or to be as intelligent as he was, when that somebody was only an inspector, for he said curtly:

'I'm going to interrogate the Mouse.'

'Ah?'

He, Lognon, had done that a dozen times, and he had the advantage of having known the tramp a long time.

'You don't think that the envelope . . .? Now I come to think about it, I seem to remember that there were some sums on it in pencil . . .'

He suddenly became aware of an infraction of all the laws of hospitality.

'You'll have a drink, won't you, Chief-Inspector? A little calvados? . . . No? . . . A glass of beer then?'

Lucas was cowardly. He didn't have the courage to drink some poor-quality beer, which was sure not to be iced, after the admirable beer of the Castiglione.

'No, thank you . . . Take it easy . . . Don't worry about anything . . . In a few days . . .'

Yes, he knew! In a few days, Chief-Inspector Lucas, with all the resources at his disposal, would have solved the mystery. His photograph would once again be published on the front page of all the papers. And nobody would talk about Inspector Lognon, of the Municipal Police.

'Good-bye, old chap . . .'

When the door closed again, Lognon almost felt like crying. In the dining-room the Mouse was still sitting on his chair, opposite the little boy who was playing with a broken toy train. Madame Lognon, in the kitchen, was doing her ironing, and she must have left the iron too long on something, for there was a smell of burning.

'You come along with me. Good-bye, Madame Lognon. Take good care of him.'

They went down, the chief-inspector and the tramp, in the same lift, where they could not help touching each other. Just as the lift reached the ground floor, the Mouse asked with a forced smile, as if he were making a joke:

'Are you arresting me?'

And the chief-inspector, without batting an eyelid, retorted:

'Perhaps!'

Chapter Seven
The Softening-up

In the taxi, the chief-inspector gave the impression of having completely forgotten the existence of the tramp, who had sat down facing him, on the folding seat, although there was room for him next to the police officer.

The Mouse kept a wary eye on him. He knew the police. He knew by heart all the stories they told about interrogations at Police Headquarters and the famous room of the spontaneous confessions. He wondered whether they would try a sandwich-and-glass-of-beer routine on him, or whether Lucas would try to get what he wanted by softening him up.

Not only did he have the theoretical side of the subject at his fingertips, but he had been interrogated hundreds of times, by gendarmes when he had been in the country – and they were the worst of all – by chief-inspectors in small towns, and by Paris police officers of all sorts: gloomy ones like Lognon, jolly ones who dug their elbows into your ribs, and others who made no distinction between one man and another and held out their tobacco pouch to you straight away.

The journey across Paris was all too short, and all of a sudden they were in front of the huge porch of the Quai des Orfèvres. For all that there was sunshine in the courtyard, and a red, white and blue flag over the main entrance, the Mouse still felt rather overawed, and this gave him some idea how he would have been affected if he had been a young offender.

Lucas paid the driver, went in under the arch, turned left, and only looked round at the foot of the stairs, as if he had forgotten his companion.

'Follow me,' he said, unnecessarily as it happened, since the Mouse was following him anyway.

And he went nimbly up the steps, pushed open the door of Police Headquarters, on the first floor, and shook hands with two men who were strolling along the corridor – two barristers, the Mouse thought.

'Has the Chief asked for me?' he said to the office messenger.

'A good quarter of an hour ago . . .'

The sunshine, which was coming through a skylight, was throwing patches of light on the benches, which were upholstered in red velvet, as at the Castiglione.

'Take this fellow to No. 3 . . .'

It was as if he attached no importance to the tramp. He hung his hat on a coat-stand and knocked on the Director's padded door, and the Mouse, who would have liked to stay, was forced to follow the office messenger, who had taken a big key out of his drawer.

'This way . . . Mind the step . . .'

As a regular patron of police-station cells, the Mouse was dazzled by a little room with newly white-washed walls and a real window looking out on an inner courtyard. There was an iron bedstead in one corner, a table and a chair.

The messenger hesitated, and asked casually, more out of habit than anything else:

'You haven't any weapons on you, have you?'

And the door closed behind him. The Mouse sat down on the edge of the bed, rested his chin on his folded hands, and suddenly, in spite of himself, started trembling.

'There was a lunch at the Ministry of the Interior,' the

Director of Police Headquarters told Lucas. 'The gentlemen there talked about the case . . .'

The gentlemen in question were, by and large, all the leading political personalities, the ministers, the deputies, possibly some ambassadors too.

'It's beginning to look rather like a music-hall turn . . . A third Swiss, exactly like the others, except that he's stiffer and better dressed, has arrived from London by the plane from Croydon . . . He's another of the gentlemen of the Basle Group, and he's shut himself up with the other two in Loëm's suite . . .'

Lucas said jokingly:

'We must wait till all twelve of them are there . . . Because there are twelve of them, aren't there?'

'I don't know if there are twelve or thirteen of them, but what I do know, because the Minister has told me, is that they're a hell of a nuisance. You mustn't forget that their President, Edgar Loëm, who is also the major stock-holder, isn't officially dead. So it's impossible to open his will. It's also impossible, under the articles, to elect anybody to take his place. And there seems to be no reason why this situation shouldn't continue indefinitely . . . I gather that on the stock market in Paris as well as in London, Brussels and Amsterdam, this mystery is affecting the price of the shares of a good dozen companies . . .'

'My instructions?' asked Lucas, who did not appear to be tremendously impressed.

'To find the corpse at all costs, but still observing the same discretion . . .'

Lucas did not smile. He returned to his office, where two inspectors were waiting to talk to him about the other case, that of the little boy who had been murdered in the suburbs.

'If he beats me up,' thought the Mouse, who was now looking out of the window at the empty courtyard, 'I'll threaten to complain to the papers. And to begin with I can always refuse to answer unless they give me a lawyer . . . A woman lawyer for preference. That would be more fun, and the papers would talk about it now . . .'

He was hot. He was thirsty. He was talking to himself like this to keep his spirits up, for he kept being affected by terrible nameless fears. He tried to make out the sounds of the building, but apart from footsteps now and then on the stairs, none reached his ears.

He saw a police van come into the courtyard. The driver got down and went out of his field of vision, and the Mouse thought to himself that it was him they had come for, to take him to prison.

It seemed to him that he had been shut up for two hours at least. Why hadn't he been interrogated yet? Oh, he knew why! A café waiter who had peddled cocaine had spent two days and two nights without seeing anybody, in the depths of winter, and he hadn't even been given anything to eat. When he had finally been taken into the chief-inspector's office, there had been a huge sandwich and a glass of beer on a tray. But it had been the chief-inspector who had eaten and drunk while questioning him.

They might do that to him. Or else they might soften him up as the saying went: in other words question him gently, pleasantly, telling him that they only wanted to help him out of a mess, that in his own interests it would be best to . . . The whole routine . . .

Then, as soon as you came clean, thinking that that would be the end of it, they changed their tune, and shoved you in the clink.

Suddenly he rushed at the door, for he saw that the daylight was beginning to fade and he was afraid of staying like that all night. He beat on it with his fists, and kicked at it. Nobody replied, and the Mouse, contrary to his habits, reeled off a whole string of terrible oaths.

What exactly did Chief-Inspector Lucas know? And above all, what did he think the tramp knew?

With Lognon it was easy. The Mouse played with him on an equal footing. But with the chief-inspector?

It was only at eight o'clock that the door opened and an inspector came in and asked:

'What do you want to eat?'

'Isn't the chief-inspector there any more?'

'Oh, he went off ages ago.'

'Isn't he coming back?'

'Not today, anyway . . . So what do you want to eat? Ham? Sausage?'

'I prefer sausage . . .'

'White wine, red wine?'

'Red.'

He was left alone again: then the door opened and the inspector, who had his hat on and must have done the shopping himself, put some packets on the table: three splendid slices of ham, a good six inches of salami – real salami from an Italian shop – two bottles of red wine and a Camembert.

'There you are. When you want to turn the light out, you'll find a switch near the bed . . .'

'Listen, Inspector . . .'

'Yes?'

'You wouldn't have a paper on you?'

He had one in his pocket, the latest edition, and he gave it to the tramp. It was almost too easy. And too luxurious. The Mouse ate all the same, consumed with a sort of fury: he ate everything, the ham, the salami, the Camembert, looking through the paper at the same time.

In the classified advertisements, in the same place as the day before, he found the appeal to Archibald.

So the murderers knew that Lognon wasn't their man. Probably they had knocked him out only because he was becoming a nuisance with his stubbornness. The man they wanted to see at Fouquet's was the Mouse. And probably, on the evening of 23 June, they had caught a glimpse of him.

They must be under the impression that the old man wanted to keep the wallet and its contents for himself. In that case, people who hadn't hesitated to murder Loëm in the centre of Paris would not recoil from a fresh crime . . .

If it wasn't for the presbytery . . .

But no! Apart from the fact that Lucas would promise not to prosecute the tramp but would lock him up all the same, perhaps even for being an accessory to murder.

He slept badly. The building was full of strange noises. People kept going up and down the staircase, as if it were broad daylight. And there was a telephone somewhere which rang every ten minutes.

In the morning, the police van was still in the courtyard, but the horse had been unharnessed.

It was harnessed at eight o'clock, and the van stayed there, half in the shade, half in the sun.

It was the office messenger he had seen the previous day who came and opened the door, yawning at the same time.

'What do you want to eat?'

'I want to speak to the chief-inspector,' protested the Mouse.

'The chief-inspector hasn't arrived yet.'

'When he does arrive, tell him that I've got to speak to him . . .'

'You don't want to eat something while you're waiting?'

This time they bought him some croissants, some white coffee in a bottle, and a few lumps of sugar in a piece of paper.

The window did not open. The sunlight was pouring right into the cell, and the Mouse, finding the heat trying, took off his jacket and his shoes.

He lay down, got up again, went and pressed his ear against the door. Then he made sure that the police van was still there. At midday, the chief-inspector had still given no sign of life, and this time, without asking him to choose his menu, they brought him a parcel of food even bigger than the previous evening, together with two bottles of red wine.

As he had done the day before, he ate it all, filled with a spirit of vengeance. He drank all the wine too, fell asleep, and awoke with a start when the sun was still high in the sky.

He felt that he was falling really ill. He had not satisfied his natural needs for twenty-four hours, and he couldn't see any place for that. The red wine and the meat were turning his stomach.

He could have sworn they had done it on purpose. He even wondered whether there might not be a little hole in the wall through which they were spying on him.

He rushed at the door again in a fit of temper. It was all right for them to use tricks like that on other people, on real murderers. But not on him. Not on a man who, so to speak, had lived on friendly terms with the police for ten years.

The man responsible was Lucas, and the Mouse hated him more every minute. In his mind's eye the chief-inspector's face was contorted, taking on a cunning, sly look. Was he even capable of smiling? He was a brute, not a good sort like Lognon, who just rolled his eyes at you and wiggled his bushy eyebrows.

It was always like that. Lognon got a savage blow on the head. He might die from it. And it was the other man who would pretend to be the smart one if anything was discovered, and who might even be decorated.

The fact remained that Lognon had been cleverer than all the rest. The Mouse knew something about that. After all, it was the Mouse, and he alone, who knew the truth.

Nobody else could boast of having seen the corpse. He could go to see them, those gentlemen from Basle the papers were talking about, and say to them:

'Buy me the presbytery and give me a small pension . . . I'll tell everything . . . Or if you prefer, if it suits you better, I'll say nothing . . .'

He had them where he wanted them. But it was no use Lucas thinking he could make him talk. Not even with piles of meat and bottles of wine galore.

Could they sentence him to more than one year? No. Well then? Provided he kept his mouth shut, he could come out to find the envelope and the dollars, which Lost Property would be obliged to hand over to him.

He was suffocating. Perhaps that was a trick of theirs too. And that horse which had been harnessed since the morning to the police van and which every now and then stamped on the paving-stones with its hooves. Why harness it if they weren't going to use it?

'Get your things,' the office messenger said all of a sudden, opening the door.

'Is the chief-inspector there?'

'I don't know.'

He had to put his shoes and jacket on again, muttering at the same time:

'You'll see what a telling-off I'm going to give your chief-inspector!'

He went on talking to himself while going up the staircase, and then while waiting in the ante-room with the skylight, where four or five gentlemen were standing chatting in a corner.

He tried to hear what they were saying. It seemed impossible to him that anybody could talk about anything but his case. Finally a door opened. A young man spotted the Mouse and said:

'Come in!'

He went in, and the young man disappeared, leaving him alone near a desk behind which Chief-Inspector Lucas was installed.

'Sit down . . . I hope you haven't gone short of anything?'

There was no denying that the real Lucas didn't look like the grimacing picture which the tramp had ended up by painting of him. To read, he put on a pair of spectacles which gave him a fatherly look. He was glancing through a file, with an interested expression on his face.

'Well I never! You know, you used to be a very respectable citizen! It says here that you were the choir-master in your village, then the organist, then a teacher of the harmonium in Strasburg. What made you give all that up? Wine?'

The Mouse wriggled for a moment on his chair, and, unable to repress a feeling of pride, murmured with false modesty:

'Mainly women . . .'

'You had an affair?'

'Several . . . And you know, even now, at my age, it's all because of a woman that I'm here . . . Anybody else, in my place, finding a photo of a girl, would have left it where it was . . . But I had to get interested in her.'

He found it hard to conceal his joy. It seemed to him that the chief-inspector, without meaning to, had just shown him what course to adopt. He only had to stick to that explanation and he would be all right.

'No convictions,' continued Lucas, who did not look up once at the tramp, but kept turning over papers which the other would have dearly liked to read. 'For somebody who has been on the tramp for so many years, that's pretty rare . . . I suppose that all the same you've got a few thefts of hens and rabbits on your conscience!'

'Like everybody else,' retorted the Mouse.

'Yes, like everybody else . . .'

An inspector came in and put another file on the desk.

'In a minute,' the chief-inspector said to him. 'Let me finish with this fellow. I'd forgotten about him and he must be in a hurry to get out into the fresh air again . . .'

So they were going to let him go! Besides, Lucas talked about his case as if it were a matter of no importance.

It was odd. The Mouse had sometimes amused a whole cellful of people by giving an imitation of a 'softening-up'. He knew the technique better than anybody else, and yet it never occurred to him that the police officer was playing with him, and that the inspector had come in only when Lucas had called him by unobtrusively pressing a button.

'Tell the others to wait for me . . .'

He looked at his watch and went on:

'Let's see . . . It's seven o'clock . . . I'll come along in ten minutes . . . Send a telephone message to Staori that I shan't be seeing him tonight . . . And let my wife know that we'll be dining in town . . .'

He came back to his tramp only regretfully, and seemed to be hunting in vain through the file for what there could be against him.

'Well, I see that you've answered all the questions you've been asked . . . Lognon must have had some theory, but I can't imagine what . . .'

'Inspector Lognon is a bit stubborn . . .'

'Ah?'

'Just between the two of us, he lacks education . . . So that he goes full-tilt after the first idea that occurs to him . . .'

'Listen, Mouse. You're a good sort, aren't you? You've never been to prison, and you don't want to go there, do you? I've been landed with an awkward case which concerns some important foreign personalities . . . You know the law?'

'What law?'

Lucas pretended to look through the Code and became a little flustered.

'Article Number I can't remember what . . . It doesn't matter . . . Any citizen who witnesses a crime, or conceals anything from the law appertaining to a crime, automatically renders himself the accomplice of the culprits and must be prosecuted as such . . . Wait till I find the place . . . It must carry a sentence of up to five years' imprisonment . . . As I was saying . . .'

The Mouse was becoming suspicious.

'As I was saying, if you knew something, as Inspector Lognon insinuates, you wouldn't fail to make a complete statement to us . . . Am I wrong?'

'No.'

The chief-inspector glanced at his watch and showed a certain impatience. He got up as if he had already finished.

'That poor fellow Lognon told me a complicated story about a certain Archibald . . . I couldn't make head or tail of it . . . Do you know a chap called Archibald?'

'No.'

'To begin with, it isn't even a name . . . I ask you, who's going to call himself Archibald? . . . Why not Alcibiades or Sesostris?'

He laughed, and the Mouse made an effort to laugh, too, to humour him. There was a knock at the door. It was the same inspector as before.

'There's a lady asking for you . . .'

The chief-inspector turned to the tramp and murmured: 'I'll be back in a moment . . .'

And the Mouse was left on his own. He resisted the temptation to lean across the desk and have a look at the famous file. That, too, might have been a trick like those which he described so well, but as soon as he himself was involved he lost all his old flair.

On top of the papers, a newspaper was lying open at the

classified advertisements page, and one of the advertisements was surrounded with a thick line in blue pencil.

'*Archibald* . . .'

The chief-inspector came back into the room while the tramp was still holding the paper. He showed neither surprise nor anger. On the contrary . . .

'Why, that gives me an idea,' he said good-humouredly. 'So much the worse for my dinner in town . . . We'll just have to go to the theatre without eating . . .'

He made a show of arguing with himself and of approving his decision.

'Why not? . . . Listen . . . The police have been putting you up for nothing every night long enough for you to do them a little service in return . . . I hope at least you've been well treated here? . . . Lognon is obsessed with this advertisement . . . He insists that it conceals heaven knows what mystery, and I've no option but to see what lies behind it . . . If I send one of my men, he'll be spotted straight away . . . We're going to go there together . . . You'll hold the *New York Herald*, and you'll go from one table to another as if you were practising your profession . . . What's the matter with you?'

'With me? . . . Nothing!'

'An hour from now you'll be as free as air . . . Wait a minute . . .'

The chief-inspector put his hat on, and called a colleague to whom he gave some orders in a low voice.

'Come along . . . We'll get the taxi to stop a couple of hundred yards from Fouquet's . . . You aren't frightened, I hope?'

Dry-mouthed, the Mouse asked:

'You don't think they'll do anything to me, do you?'

'Who? In any case two of my inspectors will be keeping an eye on you . . .'

'What shall I say?'

'Nothing at all . . . When somebody speaks to you, that'll be the fellow we're looking for . . .'

'I haven't had my dinner,' the tramp objected awkwardly.

'Nor have I. But we'll have something to eat afterwards, on our way back . . .'

He had been well and truly caught by a 'softening-up'. And by Lucas who now, in the taxi, no longer bothered to smile – by Lucas who asked sternly:

'What are you shaking like that for? Anybody would think that you had something on your conscience!'

'First of all we have to find out whether he recognized the child,' said the gentleman from Basle with the skin like orange peel. 'If you agree, I'll go and see that woman. I'll offer her an annuity of, say, fifteen francs.'

'I think it would be best to wait until the will is opened,' replied Oosting, whose cigar had over an inch of ash on it, for he was holding it carefully between two podgy fingers.

'How long does it take in France to obtain a declaration to the effect that somebody has disappeared?' asked the member of the trio who had come from London, where he represented the interests of the Group.

'I'll be seeing our lawyer this evening. I imagine it will take a year . . .'

'And what if he weren't dead?'

Then Oosting, contrary to his habits, contrary to all the traditions, not only of his family, but also of the Group, lost his temper and banged his fist down on the table, sacrificing his magnificent ash.

'But that corpse must be somewhere!'

Keeping calmer, the gentleman from London murmured:

'The corpse might possibly disappear . . . But the car! . . . Incidentally, I saw a letter just now from the garage, claiming compensation for the car . . . Fifty thousand francs . . .'

'Give them twenty thousand. It isn't worth more than

that . . . Or rather, don't give them anything . . . The risk must be covered by the insurance . . .'

The three men were not in a gay mood. They had completed the inventory of all the papers found at the Hôtel Castiglione. They had overlooked nothing, not even the stamp collection, which they had entrusted in the afternoon to an expert.

The question of knowing whether or not Loëm had a large sum of money on him at the time of his disappearance was one of the most difficult to solve, for, apart from his numerous bank accounts, the financier always kept a certain amount of currency available, in the same piece of furniture, as it happened, in which he kept his stamps.

They had found ten five-hundred-dollar notes there and eight thousand-franc notes. Müller, who came and went with noiseless tread, like a model employee, could not say whether the desk usually contained more than that.

His own fate had been settled. His passage had been booked on the boat which sailed for China on 12 July.

He was not being struck off the Group's staff, but he was being sent away – whether temporarily or for ever was something only these gentlemen knew or would decide.

They had occasionally met in the lounge a stranger with a matt complexion, who spoke with a pronounced accent, but they had not even wondered who he was. They were determined to ignore Staori and his daughter, who, in Berlin, was spending her time at the post office, waiting for letters.

'Think carefully. Don't answer straight away. You are sure that she can't do anything against the Company?' Müller had been asked, in a tone which revealed all the gravity of the situation. 'She can't have obtained access to certain documents in your office? You didn't communicate any dangerous secrets to her?'

'None, apart from Monsieur Loëm's liaison, which I

117

mentioned to her because he always considered her with a certain contempt . . .'

'Think it over. Give us your answer this evening.'

Müller had just given it. It was:

'No.'

And the gentlemen from Basle knew that he was telling the truth, that there was nothing to fear from that quarter. Consequently he could go to China and those petty schemers Staori and his daughter could be safely ignored.

'Tomorrow you'll attend to that woman, Gade.'

That woman was Lucile Boisvin.

'Before seeing her, go to the local town hall to find out about the boy . . .'

A storm was brewing. The sky had clouded over. The curtains were billowing out behind the open windows and it was dark enough for lamps to be lighted everywhere.

But the three men, sunk in their armchairs, went on smoking in the half-light, as quiet and discreet as their conversation.

The taxi drew up opposite the *Jour* building on the Champs-Élysées just as the first drops of rain, as big as five-franc pieces, started thudding on to the asphalt. At the same time a gust of wind blew down the avenue, tousling the hair of a few passers-by, and fine eddies of dust swirled along the ground.

Lucas, who, from his seat, could see the terrace of Fouquet's, stayed in the car, after saying to the Mouse:

'Off you go . . .'

He was rather worried. True, in one corner of the terrace, he had spotted one of his young inspectors, whose photograph had not yet appeared in the papers, and who was consequently unknown to the underworld.

But the shower had disturbed the customers, who were falling back to take shelter under the awning. The result was a scramble in which the Mouse, with his paper in his hand, could easily go unnoticed.

Never had the old man dragged his left leg so much. If he bent down to pick up some already wet cigarette end, it was by a miracle of intuition or habit.

What could he do? He knew that the chief-inspector had taken his precautions. Whatever happened, he had to wander along the terrace, and his only hope was that the murderers, as had happened two days before with Lognon, should think it wiser not to show themselves.

He had thought of holding the paper in such a way that the title would not show, but that was a trick which would not work with Lucas.

Another few yards . . . It was a little as if he had jumped into the water . . . He bore down on the tables and said for the first time:

'You wouldn't have a couple of francs for me to go and have a beer?'

The proof that it was the tone of voice which did the trick, especially in that business, was that from three tables he did not obtain a single franc. Admittedly the customers were more concerned about the storm and the problem of how to get home if the rain continued. The commissionaire was having a hard time stopping those taxis which had not been hired and which were hurriedly putting up their hoods.

'You wouldn't have a couple of francs for me?'

He looked into the customers' faces, and sometimes he drew back involuntarily as if he were afraid of being hit over the head like Inspector Lognon.

Why not? And what if they simply wanted to kill him off to prevent him from talking?

'Excuse me, ladies and gents . . . Forty sous for a poor tramp who hasn't had a drink for two days . . . A poor tramp who hasn't had a drink for two days . . .'

This time he got his forty sous. He had already spotted

the young inspector, who lacked the elegance of the regular patrons of the establishment. But was he somebody from the police or one of the murderers?

He was getting near the end. He was about to go into the Avenue George V where, since Lucas could not see him, he intended to quicken his pace so as to get away.

Two men were sitting at a small table. They let the old man approach without showing the slightest interest in him. Near them some people were standing waiting for a taxi. The Mouse was about to walk past.

It was done in a flash. So quickly that he didn't realize what was happening. It was the first time that anybody had put handcuffs on him, and it made a sinister impression on him to hear the lock fasten on his wrists, to feel a hard tug which shook the whole of his arm.

'Police!' was all that one of the two men had said as he pushed aside the crowd.

They literally dragged away the old man, who, panic-stricken, looked around him, seeking in vain for some protection.

A few seconds later he had crossed the pavement, and was practically thrown on to the back seat of a car whose door was slammed shut.

One of the two men was on his right, the other on his left. The car drove off, and already the customers at Fouquet's had virtually lost all interest in the incident.

Only one woman, who must have had some sort of job in films, murmured:

'All the same, what brutes they are!'

Chapter Eight
The Night on the Telephone

Water was streaming along the asphalt of the Champs-Élysées, and a sky which itself was as grey as a puddle of water was reflected in it. There were no colours or half-tones left: just black and white, black silhouettes running along the banks formed by the pavements, and black cars sailing along the river of the roadway.

The man who was sitting on the Mouse's right and who had put the handcuffs on him bent forward, opened the window which separated him from the driver, and told the latter:

'Faster, Lili! Step on it!'

For a policeman had just given the traffic the signal to stop at the Rond-Point. The car drove on. They heard three or four whistle blasts which were meant to be peremptory but which finished on a comic note, for some water had got into the policeman's whistle.

'The quays, Lili!'

The man was dark, sturdy and muscular, with the broken nose of a boxer. As calm as if he had just finished a quiet game of cards, he was attending to everything, looking ahead, looking back, and examining the Mouse, who had tried two or three times to turn round.

'Look here, you old bastard, is it possible that you didn't come alone?'

Lili, the driver, must have been barely nineteen. Arriving opposite the Louvre, he slowed down to ask for orders.

'Carry on . . . Get out of Paris any way you like . . .'

And the man with the broken nose stared hard at the Mouse, then looked back at the cars following them.

'Didn't you hear my question? I asked you whether you were alone . . .'

'Yes, of course.'

'You look to me as if you're lying.'

In fact the Mouse could scarcely hear and was answering automatically, he was so intent upon coming to a decision straight away. The time had come when his fate was going to be decided, when he would have to defend, not only his presbytery, but possibly his skin as well.

The car swerved from side to side, grazed a tram, skidded on the Place du Châtelet, and straightened out miraculously, while Lili remained imperturbable at the wheel and the boxer went on thinking.

'I can't see anybody,' murmured Broken Nose's companion after taking a long look through the rear window.

'Keep on looking . . . What about that taxi?'

'It's come from the Rue de Rivoli.'

'You're sure?'

'Positive. I saw it come out near the Samaritaine . . .'

Was Chief-Inspector Lucas behind or wasn't he? That was the first question the Mouse asked himself. Next he had to decide what was the best thing to say. That the police had set a trap and that the old man, without wanting to, had served as bait?

That was dangerous. The fellow on his right was a tough egg, who wouldn't hesitate to take extreme measures. Already they had crossed Paris at record speed and were approaching the Porte d'Italie. If the two men believed that they were being pursued, there would be a wild chase along the slippery road, probably with shots from both sides . . .

'You're sure there weren't any cops around you?'

'I didn't see any,' replied the Mouse, putting all the innocence of which he was capable into his voice.

The other apparently believed him. He grunted:

'We'll see . . .'

Then he said to Lili:

'Keep on driving . . . Go around Paris and back into the city by way of Saint-Denis or Pantin . . .'

'My wrists are hurting,' groaned the tramp, whose skin was being bruised by the handcuffs. 'Don't you belong to the police?'

'Don't play the idiot, you old bastard!'

Trees, fields, under the driving rain. The old tramp looked sadly at a cow standing at the roadside.

He was not particularly frightened of his companion on the left. Moreover, he had the impression that he had met him fairly often on the Champs-Élysées.

Unlike the boxer, he was tall and flabby, with thinning hair, and dressed with a seedy aristocratic elegance which had earned him the nickname of the Count. He did not seem very much more at ease than the old man, and every time he turned towards the inside of the car, the other man called him to order:

'Look behind!'

'We can't be being followed . . .'

'Now you, answer my questions!'

Broken Nose was going to concentrate his attention on the Mouse. The car was still moving. The back of Lili, who was lighting a cigarette from an electric lighter, didn't budge.

'The wallet . . .'

'What wallet?'

The old man had not yet come to a decision. What he would have liked to know first of all was whether Lucas was behind or not. But how, with a mere taxi, could anybody follow a car which had threaded its way through the traffic in defiance of all regulations, and which was still travelling at sixty miles an hour over a surface as shiny as a pond?

'Listen, Fred,' said Lili, who was talking without turning round.

'I'm listening.'

'What if we drove him around for another half-hour before going back into town? . . . You get me? . . . In case we have to give the old boy a real going-over and we need to get rid of him . . .'

He had said this with the cigarette still stuck to his lower lip, in a normal voice, and his companion thought carefully before giving his approval.

'Right!'

If the Count seemed nervous, the other two appeared perfectly calm, and the one Lili had just called Fred suddenly pinched the Mouse's arm and asked:

'Where's the wallet?'

'I assure you . . . Oh!'

'Haven't you understood yet? . . . You think we're going to be satisfied with your little act? . . . But first of all, why didn't you come sooner?'

'I don't know . . .'

'You hadn't read the advert?'

'No.'

'Was it you who blabbed to the inspector?'

'To Inspector Lognon? Not on your life! If you think that, you're completely wrong . . .'

Seeing that there was no car behind . . . It was dark now. There could be nothing less reassuring than the section of moving landscape lit up by the headlamps.

Ever since Lili's remark, the Mouse had been unable to get rid of a certain mental picture: he saw the car stopping somewhere, preferably near a small wood, and Fred, helped by Lili, taking his body to throw it into a thicket, where it might not be found for weeks.

Wasn't that the way they had got rid of Loëm? And didn't the papers often mention old men who had been found like that in the woods?

The Mouse was terribly frightened and yet he could not bring himself to abandon the idea of his presbytery for good.

'What have you done with the wallet?'

'It isn't me!' he replied at the very moment that Fred pinched him savagely. 'You're hurting me!' he growled, 'Please don't hurt me any more...'

He turned automatically towards the Count, guessing that on that side there was a certain uneasiness, possibly pity.

"Tell him to leave me alone, monsieur. If I knew anything I'd talk. Everybody's been pestering me with this business for over a week now ... I swear to you that you're wrong ... What reason would a poor man like me have for lying?'

Every time he caught sight of a village or a car, his heart started pounding wildly. He was close to people who were free. All he needed was a trifling accident, a break-down, a shortage of petrol ...

The Count must have given his companion a reproachful look, for Fred said simply:

'I tell you I recognize him! You don't think I'm going to let an old bastard like him take me in, do you? Lili!'

'Yes?'

'Drive home ... It'll be easier to have a little chat there...'

He settled himself comfortably in the corner of the seat, lit a cigarette, and confined himself to uttering a few words from time to time.

'Think it over ... Take your time ... But, remember, that you'll have to talk in the end ...'

There was a long silence. They were coming back into Paris by way of the Porte de Charenton. The Count was still looking out of the rear window. And Fred must have been thinking, for he asked his companion:

'You're sure you didn't see any coppers you knew around Fouquet's?'

'I'd have said so . . .'

'All right.'

But Fred wasn't satisfied. He was in a surly mood, and seemed to be chewing over an unpleasant suspicion. In Paris he himself took over the watch through the rear window and told Lili to carry out several detours. Finally the car drew up right at the top of the Rue Blanche.

'You see to the car, Lili.'

'Right.'

'As for you, if you so much as open your trap . . .'

And Fred pushed his knife a quarter of an inch into the old man's thigh, by way of a warning.

The car, which had been stolen that very evening outside a cinema in the Rue du Colisée, was abandoned in the Boulevard Rochechouart. Then Lili came quietly back to the Rue Blanche on foot, with the rain falling in a gentle drizzle, as if it were going to last all night. Lili installed himself in a bar at the corner of the street, from which he could see the door of the apartment-house which the other three had entered.

As for the Mouse, he was stark naked. And anybody would have thought that he was going to burst out sobbing any moment.

The flat consisted of only two rooms and a cubby-hole which served as a kitchen. The Count was eating some bread and ham he had taken out of a cupboard, and pretending to take no interest in what was going on.

As it was still hot, in spite of the rain, and they had had to shut the windows, Fred had taken off his jacket. With the minute care of an expert in the Police Records Department, he had examined the tramp's clothes seam by seam, carrying thoroughness to the extent of slitting open the soles of his shoes and tearing the heels off.

There was very little furniture in the room: a bed, a table, some chairs, and a wardrobe with a mirror. The flat was obviously rented furnished, and next door there was a little sitting-room with some armchairs upholstered in faded tapestry and a sordid carpet.

An alarm clock on the bedside-table registered ten past eleven when Fred got up with a sigh from his chair and went over to the Mouse, who raised his arm to protect himself, but too late. The other man had driven his fist into the middle of his face, making his nose bleed and his left eyelid swell up.

'You're a stubborn bastard, aren't you! How far do I have to go to make you understand? . . . Can't you explain to him, Count, that we didn't go to all that trouble for his sake . . . The Wallet!'

The fist rose again. At the sight of his own blood, the Mouse felt faint.

'Wait . . . I'll tell you . . .'

'About time, too . . . Go on . . .'

'Well the fact is . . . I don't know where it is . . .'

'What's that?'

'No . . . Wait a minute . . . That's the truth . . . I don't know where it is at present . . . I didn't dare to keep it on me, seeing that I sleep every night in the cells and they sometimes search me . . .'

'Where is it?'

'Under . . . under the seat of a coach that does the race-courses . . .'

Fred frowned, while the Count stopped eating.

'What coach?'

'I'll show it to you tomorrow . . .'

'Bloody hell! You think you're going to get away with

that? You just wait, you little bastard – I'll make you talk...'

The Mouse could not stand it any longer. He was disgusted with Lucas, who had let him down like that and left him at the mercy of the murderers.

'Wait a minute... I give you my word of honour it's the truth... It's a blue coach, an old one, that's garaged at the Porte Maillot... There's a drawing of a stork on the bonnet...'

'I've seen a coach like that,' said the Count.

'You're sure? Then get over to the Porte Maillot... Cook up some story for the watchman at the garage...'

Obviously relieved, the Count picked up his hat and made for the door.

'Just a minute,' cried the Mouse, who was scared of being left alone with the brutal Fred.

'What now?'

'The wallet's empty... Or nearly...'

'Get along with you!'

They didn't believe him. The Count, with his hat on his head, and his hand on the latch, waited, chewing the last mouthful of his sandwich.

'What did you do with what was inside?'

'I handed it over to Lost Property...'

'To Lost Property...'

Fred did not understand, frowned, and got up, ready to hit the tramp again, but the Count intervened.

'Wait a minute... Perhaps he's telling the truth...'

'Then he'd better explain!'

'I didn't dare keep so much money... I'd have been arrested... I persuaded the police that I'd found it... Like that, if nobody claims it within a year...'

It was a pity, but it couldn't be helped. He had to save his skin now. He had to avoid any fresh blows, and get out of this room from which it seemed to him that he would never emerge alive.

And yet, in spite of everything, he had not abandoned all hope. The gangsters would not dare to go to Lost Property to collect the bank-notes. Who could tell whether. . .?

'You've decided to come clean, have you?' growled Fred, who perhaps had also had enough.

'I swear I'll tell you the whole truth!'

'Well, well . . . Put your trousers on . . . You're an eyesore like that . . .'

He threw him his clothes and went over to him, not to hit him, but to take his handcuffs off.

'Remember that you'll lose nothing by waiting . . . Wipe your nose . . . Count, give him a wet towel.'

The Mouse made the mistake of thinking that the time had come to put on his little act again, and, already more at ease now that he was dressed, he murmured:

'If you'd told me straight away that you were gentlemen, and that . . .'

'None of your clap-trap . . . Explain . . . What did you hand over to Lost Property?'

'The dollars which I'd slipped into an envelope.'

'All of them?'

He was tempted to cheat, but the look in Fred's eyes stopped him.

'All except one note of each sort . . . You understand? Like that, if anybody had claimed the money, he wouldn't have been able to say the right amount and they wouldn't have given him the envelope . . .'

He winked pitifully. It was not working.

'And what did you do with the other things?'

'What other things? There was only a photo and three tickets to Luna Park . . . It was Inspector Lognon who pinched the photo from me . . . In fact, that was how it all started . . .'

'And the letter?'

T – T.M. – E

'There wasn't any letter . . . I swear to you – and this time I'm telling the truth – that the envelope was empty . . .'

'You threw it away?' cried Fred in sudden anxiety.

'No . . . It's still in the wallet . . .'

Fred drew the Count into a corner and spoke to him for a moment in an undertone. Then the Count went off, leaving the two men alone together.

The Mouse was beginning to regain confidence. He wondered how to turn the situation to his advantage.

'I'll tell you something . . . If only you'll promise not to do any more harm to a poor old man who hasn't got much longer to live . . .'

Fred was not listening. He had drawn the curtain aside and was looking down into the street, where they could hear the monotonous sound of the rain.

'It's about the dollars . . . The way things are, nobody can touch them . . . But I can get them back a year from now, and if you promise me a small share . . . Just enough to buy a little place in my part of the world, now that the police are hounding me all the time . . .'

Not a word from Fred, who was still looking outside. Behind the windows of the bar on the corner, he could see the silhouette of Lili, who was keeping watch. He was still calm, with a hint of uneasiness in his eyes.

'When you've finished your clap-trap,' he sighed.

'Just as you like . . . All I was saying . . .'

'Oh, shut up!' shouted Fred, who had had enough.

In spite of the late hour, they could hear a gramophone or a wireless somewhere in the building. The Mouse noticed for the first time that there was a telephone on the table in the sitting-room, and it occurred to him that if he had been nearer to it he might have been able, unobtrusively, to dial the number of the Emergency Service.

'I'm thirsty,' he said on the off-chance.

The other man pointed to the tap in the kitchen. But

there was no way out in that direction, and the Mouse had to pretend to drink some water.

Lucas, like Fred, had taken off his jacket. He had almost the same hard, sombre look in his eyes as the gangster, and he kept scolding his colleagues just as harshly.

Things had not gone quite as he hoped, that was all, and he had had to improvise, to change his tactics, so that even now, they might still lose the game.

To begin with, the kidnapping of the Mouse at Fouquet's had been carried out with remarkable speed. Admittedly a police car was parked near by, but it had scarcely had time to extricate itself from the chaotic mass of taxis.

Then there had been the storm, that torrential downpour which had played havoc with the traffic in Paris. Lili, at the wheel of a powerful car, had turned it to good advantage, indifferent as he was to the idea of knocking down a pedestrian. But the little car from Police Headquarters could not keep up the same speed.

That was why Lucas had told his driver to take him, not to the Quai des Orfèvres, but to the Prefecture of Police.

He was still there, in his shirt-sleeves, with his pipe between his teeth, in that huge room on the second floor which was like the brain of the police force, because it was linked by telegraph to every station, and a lighted board on the wall, near a telephone switchboard, kept it informed of every call made to the Emergency Service.

The three windows overlooking the courtyard were wide open, and the driving rain could be seen in the halo of light, while now and then a car could be heard hooting in the square in front of Notre-Dame.

Twice already the Director of the Municipal Police, whose flat was next door, on the same floor, and who was entertaining some friends that evening, had looked in out of curiosity to ask if there was any news. As for the Prefect, installed at the other end of the building, he was telephoning every quarter of an hour.

By now – it was ten past eleven at night – it could be said that the end was a matter of luck.

Lucas had done everything he could. He had not overlooked the least of the resources placed at his disposal.

What could be held against him – and what would undoubtedly be held against him if he failed – was that he had sacrificed the Mouse by not arresting the two men the moment they had seized the tramp on the terrace of Fouquet's.

The papers would protest indignantly, and so would what they called decent people. Only those familiar with the work of the police would understand.

Lucas, from a distance, had promptly recognized the Count, who had a record of at least four convictions, admittedly for minor offences such as passing dud cheques and committing petty frauds.

His presence in this business had in fact worried Lucas, for he thought he knew the man and he could not see him getting involved in a murder case.

The other man was a different matter, even though he had had only one conviction in France. Fred, who was a native of Sicily, had worked in America for four or five years at the time of Prohibition, and since he had been in Paris there had been nothing in particular anyone could hold against him, apart from his general manner and his friends.

If Lucas had arrested these two as soon as they had handcuffed the Mouse, what good would that have done? They were both experienced enough to keep their mouths shut. So that all he could have hoped to obtain against them, at the very best, was a sentence of three months' imprisonment, for impersonating police officers.

The Mouse had a secret. To tell the truth, the idea at the

back of Lucas's mind was that the two gangsters had means of making the old man talk, which he, as a chief-inspector of Police Headquarters, was not entitled to use.

As a famous prefect used to say, you can't keep order by using choir-boys.

And Lucas, when laying his plans, had not foreseen that the storm would break just in time to prevent his colleagues from following the car.

Since then, everything that could be done had been done, and it was not for nothing that the chief-inspector had installed his command post in this room to which so many telephone and telegraph wires were connected.

To begin with, in three minutes the number of the car had been circulated to all the police in France, so that after only a quarter of an hour the Thirteenth Arrondissement station reported seeing it at the Port d'Italie.

At half past eight, an inspector stationed himself in the lounge of a hotel in the Avenue de Wagram where the Count rented a room by the week.

Two others, in bars on the Champs-Élysées and the Étoile, questioned the staff about Fred while a sergeant went into the apartment house in the Rue Blanche and sat on the stairs, a floor above the Sicilian's flat.

Twice the gendarmes at Villeneuve-Saint-Georges reported seeing the car, which must have turned round in that district. As for the police car, incapable of doing a tour like that, it had returned to its base, and was waiting with its driver at the wheel and its four men inside.

All the police stations in Paris had not only a description of the car, but one of its occupants too. There was not a single policeman in the streets who was not staring hard at the passers-by.

And a score of vans of the Emergency Service, outside a score of stations, were waiting too, filled with policemen.

'Still no news, Prefect. They're in the neighbourhood of

Villeneuve-Saint-Georges and it looks as if they are going to come back into Paris . . .'

If they went any farther out, the gendarmes in the country had also been put on their guard, as had the small towns in the departments of Seine, Seine-et-Oise and Seine-et-Marne.

Lucas had not even eaten a sandwich. He, too, had thought of the little wood where the gangsters might throw the Mouse's lifeless body into a ditch.

Now that was a risk which had to be run. He could not do any more than he had done.

He knew that at that very moment Staori was in one of the Boulevard theatres in the company of one of his fellow-countrymen and the latter's wife, who was a magnificent creature.

As for the gentlemen from Basle, one of them – Oosting – was in bed. The one from London was in an English bar in the Rue Daunou where, contrary to all expectations, he was indulging by himself in the pleasures of whisky. As for Orange-Skin, he had quite simply taken a seat in the front row at the Folies Bergère.

This did not even bring a smile to the lips of the chief-inspector, who pushed caution to the point of making sure that Lord Archibald Landsburry was attending a reception at the Japanese Embassy.

And all this was going on under the same rain, which now looked as if it was going to last all night – rain which was cooling the air outside but which was forcing the heat of the last few days into the flats where the Parisians were finding it hard to get to sleep.

Suddenly there was a rush of telephone calls, with lamps lighting up one after another, so that the calls had to be taken on three different receivers and the Director of the Municipal Police left his guests to stand behind Lucas.

First there was Picpus, which announced that the car

had just come back into Paris by way of the Porte de Charenton, then the Quinze-Vingts station which reported it passing along the Avenue Daumesnil at a moderate speed. Finally, one after the other, came La Folie-Méricourt and the station at the Saint-Louis Hospital.

So the car was returning towards Montmartre. None of the policemen was capable of saying whether, apart from the driver, there were still three living human beings inside.

On the other hand, the last telephone call came from Sergeant Janvier, who was installed on the staircase in the Rue Blanche. The sound of a gramophone could be heard at the same time as his voice.

'I'm in the flat upstairs,' he explained, 'which belongs to a very helpful lady . . . She's playing the gramophone for me so that I can't be heard downstairs . . . Hullo . . . Are you there ? . . . They've come back . . . The car's gone off again with the driver . . . I'm going to go down on to the landing . . . Send some men !'

There was already a call from Rochechouart.

'The car has just been found, with nobody in it, near the Place d'Anvers. What shall we do with it ?'

When the Prefect telephoned from his flat, Lucas replied:

'I think we're going to manage.'

He had had nothing to eat since one o'clock in the afternoon. He drank a bottle of beer belonging to one of the telephonists who always brought along some food and drink for the night.

'One van at the corner of the Rue Mansart and the Rue Blanche,' ordered Lucas. 'Another at the corner of the Rue Moncey.'

Like that they could shut off the stretch of the Rue Blanche in which the gangsters were going to be trapped.

The order had scarcely been given before Sergeant Janvier telephoned again.

'The big fat chap has just left now . . . The old man is alone with Fred . . .'

This time they created a record. Lucas, on the off-chance, told the Saint-Georges station to send a dependable taxi close to the building. The taxi was so dependable that a plain-clothes inspector, who had exchanged his hat for a cloth cap, installed himself beside the driver, as if he were a pal of his.

Thanks to the rain, which had led to a concentration of cabs round the theatres, the taxi arrived in time and was hailed by the Count.

'The Porte Maillot!' he said, before seeing that there was somebody next to the driver.

All the same, until it was all over, they could not say the game was won. One of the inspectors who had been detailed in the afternoon, just in case, to shadow the gentlemen from Basle, telephoned proudly to report that the man with the orange-peel skin, Monsieur Gade, had yielded, during the interval at the Folies Bergère, to the persuasions of a tout who had promised him some lascivious dances on premises near the theatre, and who had taken him to a well-known brothel.

'All right,' muttered Lucas.

'Shall I go on?'

No reply.

The chief-inspector had already picked up another receiver.

'Hullo . . . He's just gone into a garage at the Porte Maillot. What do you want me to do?'

'Stay there, and after he's gone, ask the watchman what he wanted . . .'

Time drags in cases like that. Especially since Janvier was giving no further sign of life . . .

'Hullo . . . It's me again . . . He's just left, and told the taxi-driver to take him back to the Rue Blanche . . . So I didn't think it necessary to go with him . . .'

This was another report on the Count. The telephone call was from the Porte Maillot.

'The watchman is here beside me . . . He says the man asked if he could see a coach which does the race-courses and which has a stork on the bonnet . . . Well, that particular coach was sent to Vichy two days ago for the season, as it is every year . . . What do you want me to do now?'

Lucas had hung up once again and was asking for a call to be made to the chief-inspector at Vichy. He turned to one of his colleagues. 'When you've got him on the line, tell him to impound the blue coach with the stork on the bonnet and put it under lock and key . . .'

He put on his jacket and looked around for his hat.

'You and you . . . Yes, you two men, come along with me to the Rue Blanche . . .'

The little car was waiting for them in the courtyard, and the policeman on duty opened wide the doors into the square in front of Notre-Dame.

During the seven minutes which the journey through the wet streets lasted, Lucas looked as if he were dozing.

Chapter Nine
The Peregrinations of Madame Lognon

It was one of the telegraphists who, coming out of the huge room to go to the washroom, noticed a woman drifting about on the landing. For that was the impression which Madame Lognon gave, with her wet suit, her rain-sodden hat, and her frightened eyes.

'What is it?' the man asked.

'Chief-Inspector Lucas, please.'

'You must have passed him. He's just gone out . . .'

The telegraphist thought no more about the matter, so she remained standing there in the staircase well. If she had missed Lucas, it was because, for over half an hour, she had been wandering through the empty Prefecture, alone among miles of corridors lit by dim bulbs, faced with hundreds of numbered doors opening into empty offices.

Downstairs, when they had gathered who she was, they had told her:

'Take the third staircase on the left at the far side of the courtyard, behind the fence . . .'

She must have taken the wrong staircase, and when, after so much searching, she finally met a human being, he disappeared without taking any further notice of her.

'Whatever happens, deliver my letter into his own hands,' her husband had told her. He might have picked a different sort of evening to have an inspiration. All day he had refused to allow anybody to speak to him, replying simply with these words:

'I'm thinking!'

This in itself had put Madame Lognon in a bad temper. Especially as he did not think all by himself. Every moment he wanted something, a pencil, some paper, the previous day's newspaper, that of the day before, or a telephone directory which his wife had to go and fetch from a café.

Then, when the storm was almost imminent, he declared:

'You must go round and see your brother . . .'

'Francis?'

Yes, Francis, who was a school-teacher at Issy-les-Moulineaux.

'You must ask him to lend you the volume of the big Larousse containing the letter L . . .'

'You're sure it's necessary?'

'What would you say if I was transferred to Police Headquarters?'

Madame Lognon entrusted the boy to a neighbour, for his father could not stand the slightest noise.

'That blow on the head has made him more unbearable than ever . . .' she told Francis, who wrapped the book in three layers of paper.

All that just for Lognon to use it for barely five minutes, and then to start writing a letter.

'Don't take your things off . . . You must go to Police Headquarters . . . You must ask for Chief-Inspector Lucas and hand him this letter . . . If he isn't there, ask for his address . . .'

And so much the worse for their son, who had gone to bed without any dinner! At Police Headquarters, there was no Lucas, but they gave her his address, which was over near the Porte de Versailles.

There, the storm and no chief-inspector. Then Police Headquarters again, and finally this dreadful Prefecture of Police where all the corridors looked the same, and where all the staircases brought her back to the same maze. This time, she had had enough, and she sat down on the second step to rest her legs.

A quarter of an hour later, she was still there, listening automatically to the sound of telephones ringing. Then she managed to distinguish some voices, but she did not try to make out what they were saying.

Chance came to her rescue. The Director of the Municipal Police, on his way out of the building, instead of using his private staircase, went down the staircase of the Emergency Service. Opening the door, he found this woman sitting on the stairs and frowned,

'What are you doing there?'

'I've an urgent letter for Chief-Inspector Lucas.'

'Give it to me. I'm on my way to see him as it happens . . .'

But she shook her head.

'My husband, Inspector Lognon, told me to deliver it to him, into his own hands . . .'

He shrugged his shoulders and muttered:

'Come along with me . . .'

For Lucas had just telephoned to him that he was at Police Headquarters, on the Quai des Orfèvres, *with the birds*.

And, as the Prefect was anxious to have the latest news, he had sent his Director over there to find out what was happening.

Barely a dozen people had noticed anything, even though it was the time when the theatres and cinemas were emptying. Admittedly, that part of the Rue Blanche was always fairly quiet.

The principal spectators were the three men playing cards with the *patron* of the little bar in which Lili was keeping watch. At one moment, the young man had got up and shut himself in the call-box. Now, the men in the bar could hear everything through the thin partition.

'Hullo . . . Is that you, Fred? . . . Look out! . . . The cops! . . . Shall I do a bunk?'

While he was talking, two inspectors came silently into the bar, motioned to the customers to keep quiet, and listened behind the door.

'Yes, they've sent a van . . . I reckon it's the Count who's blown the gaff . . . Yes . . . O.K. . . . You can count on me . . .'

He opened the door, took in the situation at a glance, and rushed forward with such force that one of the inspectors fell on to the floor.

But the other dived at his legs and grabbed his left foot, while Lili fumbled furiously in his pocket and brought out a shiny object.

This earned him a truncheon blow full in the face which split his upper lip, after which he was handcuffed.

Fred, who was no longer eighteen, behaved in a much more dignified manner. After Lili's telephone call, he replaced the receiver calmly and looked at the Mouse, who was intrigued.

'It's nothing . . . A pal of mine,' he said. 'Wait for me a moment . . .'

Then he made for the door, which he opened, taking care not to turn on the light outside. In the darkness, without making any noise, he started going not downstairs but up. He thought he had heard some noises down below. As he went up, he quickened his pace, but suddenly he froze, for his chest had met something hard, the barrel of a revolver.

'Where are you going?' a voice asked at the same time.

'Me? . . . Where am I going? . . .'

While he was talking he had sized up the situation and come to a decision.

'Good heavens, I must have got the wrong floor. I hope I haven't hurt you?'

'Start walking downstairs . . .'

And the inspector turned the light on, removing in a familiar gesture the revolver in Fred's pocket.

The two men had gone down only a few steps when they met Lucas and two inspectors who were also lying in wait on the staircase.

It was Lucas who opened the door of the flat, after replying to a worried neighbour:

'Go back inside . . . Nothing's happening . . .'

The oddest thing was that the Mouse, who did not know what was happening, but had heard some unusual noises, had hidden behind a curtain, so that only his feet were visible.

'Come out of there!'

'At last! So you've come to set me free,' he muttered as he came out. 'And about time too! . . . What would you have said if you hadn't found me alive? . . .'

'On your way! . . . There's no need to wake up the whole house . . .'

At the most two or three doors were opened a little way . . . A few moments later, the three men were in the van, jammed between policemen. But the van did not drive off yet. It waited. Before ten minutes had gone by, a taxi drew up outside the building and two inspectors closed in on the Count as he got out.

'Full house!' announced Lucas. 'The Quai des Orfèvres . . .'

He had just telephoned to the central station where he had spent part of the evening.

'Hullo . . . Put Vichy through to me as soon as they call . . . Tell the Prefect that I'm here with my birds . . .'

It was thanks to this telephone call that Madame Lognon had been rescued from her monotonous stay on one step of a staircase. She arrived accompanied by the Director of the Municipal Police, whom she did not know and who was a wiry little man with a goatee. More stairs and corridors, all deserted, poorly lit, and smacking of the night shift.

The inspectors who had taken part in the arrests had hung up their jackets to dry. The Brasserie Dauphine had just been rung up and asked to send up some beer.

'Chief-Inspector Lucas?' asked the Director.

'In his office . . .'

He was not alone. The four men were lined up in front of him: the Mouse, Fred, the Count, and finally Lili with his split lip. Without saying anything, the Director sat down in a corner. Madame Lognon had come in behind him, and Lucas looked at her in amazement.

'What are *you* doing here?'

'I've brought a letter from my husband . . . Don't you recognize me?'

No, he didn't recognize her, and he was preoccupied with other matters.

'I'm Inspector Lognon's wife, and here's the letter . . .'

Poor woman! How she was going to catch it on her return home, when she told her husband that the chief-inspector was questioning some prisoners, including the Mouse, and that it had not even occurred to her to wait!

For she went off as she had come, noiselessly, and nearly got lost once again in the corridors . . .

Lucas read the letter through twice and automatically passed it over to the Director of the Municipal Police.

Sir,

I believe that in the solitude of my sickbed I may have penetrated the secret of Archibald which, right from the start, has struck me as the centre of this whole case at the same time as its darkest mystery.

This is what I have copied out of the Larousse Encyclopedia (1913 edition) which my brother-in-law has been kind enough to lend me:

'Sir Archibald Landsburry (1824–1887), famous English botanist.'

'Archibald C. Landsburry (1851–1914), son of the above, Viceroy of India, raised to the peerage in 1903.'

Lucas turned the page, expecting to find a lengthy explanation. But Inspector Lognon simply concluded:

In the hope that this information may be of use to you, I remain, Sir, your Obedient Servant.

Lucas put the letter on the desk, called one of his men and spoke to him in an undertone. A few minutes later, Fred, Lili and the Count were locked up in separate cells at Police Headquarters, while the Mouse was beginning to show a certain uneasiness.

'Did they beat you up?' Lucas asked in his most natural voice, pointing to the old man's nose, which was still swollen.

'If they didn't kill me, it's no fault of yours!'

'Nonsense! It would have been better if they'd knocked you about a bit more, then instead of going to prison, you'd have been taken care of in the infirmary ...'

'Prison?'

'Why, yes! You must admit that you deserve it. Didn't I speak to you, this very day, in this office, about an article in the Code concerning complicity in murder?'

For a moment, anybody would have thought that it was all over, that the tramp was going to come clean. He thought, staring at the floor, but when he raised his head again it was to murmur with a smile:

'That won't wash.'

'Just as you like. So I note that you've got nothing to say?'

'What do you expect me to say?'

'You haven't witnessed any illegal act, and you haven't taken any part whatever in actions which might tend to cover the traces of criminals?'

'I'm tired,' sighed the Mouse.

'All right . . . You'll be given a bed.'

He spoke with a deliberate sadness. He did not raise his voice. He seemed to be going half-heartedly through unimportant formalities.

' Janvier! Take the Mouse to a cell . . . See that he's given a wet towel to wash his face . . .'

He remained alone with the Director for a moment, and he allowed himself a sigh. That was enough. The two men understood each other. It was going to be difficult, very difficult . . .

Each man had a different attitude. Lili, the first to be brought in before Lucas, was mocking and insolent.

'What was I doing in the car? Why, I was just driving around. Is that a crime?'

And that was how it went with all the questions.

'Archibald? Never heard of him. What a monicker! . . .'

How did he earn his living?

'Don't you think I'm good-looking enough to make out?'

When Fred's turn came, he recited his name and personal particulars, giving his occupation as:

'Ladies' masseur and physical training instructor . . .'

Fred was calmer and his gaze was as dull as the chief-inspector's. He seemed to be saying:

' Just you try . . .'

The most amusing thing was that he kept up what might have been called a diplomatic tradition by saying:

'I'd better warn you straight away that you'll have to answer for all this to my Ambassador. Because you don't appear to realize that I'm a naturalized citizen of the United States . . .'

Just as the gentlemen from Basle had set their Minister in motion. Just as Staori had taken his to the Ministry of the Interior.

'Why did you kidnap the Mouse this evening at Fouquet's?'

'I'm not answering any questions until my lawyer's here.'

There was nothing to be done about it. He would have to wait.

There was only the Count left, though admittedly there was less swagger about him than about the others.

'As for you, my lad,' Lucas said in a different tone of voice, 'I don't recognize you any more . . . Until now I'd regarded you as an intelligent chap who, even though he did pass through my hands or my colleagues' hands now and then, had the good taste to avoid any serious risks . . .'

He was pitiful, this fat fellow, rather too well dressed, who bowed his head and searched laboriously for some excuse.

'Getting mixed up with a fellow like Fred, when a man's as well-bred as you are and knocks about in the best bars! . . . Now you're in a pretty pickle, aren't you, with a corpse on your hands?'

'What has Fred said?'

'He's come clean, of course. What else did you expect him to do? Seeing that we've found the body . . .'

'That isn't true!'

'What isn't true?'

'What you've just been saying . . . And for a start, you haven't any right to question me . . . I'll answer the examining magistrate . . .'

'Just as you like . . .'

He had foreseen that this would happen . . . Lucas knew his customers, and once they were locked up, each in a different cell, he was not very optimistic.

'Hullo . . . Hasn't Vichy asked for me yet?'

'Not yet . . .'

'Then I'm going to have a bite,' he told his companion. 'As for you, Director, you can tell the Prefect what you've seen and heard. He'll get my report tomorrow morning . . .'

A terribly difficult report to write, which he tried not to think about while he was eating some cold meat in a brasserie at the Châtelet. It was still raining, an increasingly thin, monotonous rain, and the last umbrellas of the night could be seen going past.

Soon the streets would be as deep and empty as canals . . .

'Hello . . . Yes . . . Wait while I take that down . . . One five-hundred-dollar-bill, one of one hundred, one of . . . But the envelope . . . You say it's empty? . . . I know that, dammit . . . What I'm asking you is what it's like . . . Like any other envelope? . . . Oh, it's an old one . . . A very old one . . . And you can't see anything special about it? . . . At last! You've got it! . . . No, Chief-Inspector, I'm not making fun of you . . . I'm asking you what colour the stamp is . . . Blue? . . . A Hawaiian stamp? . . . Well, that's all I wanted to know . . . You'll lock everything away, won't you . . . You've got a good safe I hope? . . .'

He turned to Sergeant Janvier, who was staying up with him.

'Go and fetch the Count!'

The latter had had his tie and his shoe-laces taken away, which robbed him of some of his elegance.

'Don't sit down . . . It isn't worth it . . . There's just something I wanted to ask you . . . You still deal in rare stamps, don't you? . . . It was you, wasn't it, who got into trouble three years ago, after the discovery of some fake stamps of some country or other?'

'The charge was dropped!'

'I don't care a damn . . . Tell me . . . Is there a Hawaiian stamp issued about the middle of the last century which is worth quite a lot? . . . Answer me! . . . No, I'm not trying to catch you out, you idiot . . . If you don't answer, I can get the information from anybody else . . .'

'There's the 1851 Hawaii, which is worth about four hundred thousand francs . . .'

'Is it blue?'

'Yes, it's blue . . . There are only about a dozen known to exist, very few of them in good condition . . .'

'Thank you, you can go back to bed . . .'

'Am I free? . . .'

'No, of course not. Back to bed in your cell . . . Incidentally . . .'

The other already had one hand on the door-handle.

'I suppose you've got nothing to tell me?'

And the Count, after hesitating for a moment, replied almost regretfully:

'No, nothing . . .'

. . . this is the complete explanation of that mysterious reference to Archibald . . .

The chief-inspector was writing his report, weighing every word. It was three o'clock in the morning. Heavy drops of water were falling on the window-sill. The Seine was flowing along under low clouds, which, every now and then, revealed a serene moon.

Janvier was asleep on a chair. The beer glasses were empty on the desk.

. . . the Count, who started work as a jobber, and who might have turned out a decent fellow, met Fred in the bars on the Champs-Élysées. Their relations were just those of men who drank apéritifs and played poker together.

Until he makes a confession, we are reduced to conjecture, but the following hypotheses seem plausible, especially as they square with the characters of the people concerned.

Edgar Loëm, whose stamp collection must be worth a fortune (the second of the gentlemen from Basle, after it had been valued, had it deposited in a bank vault) had two of the famous 1851 Hawaii blues, one of which was on an envelope addressed

148

at that time to Sir Archibald Landsburry, the English botanist, who made a study of the flora of the Pacific.

It is probable that Loëm tried to exchange his duplicate for another stamp, or even to sell it, and that he put an advertisement in a philatelic journal.

Did reading this advertisement give the Count the idea of a swindle? That seems practically certain, just as it seems certain that he spoke to Fred about it.

The plan was laid straight away. Negotiations were opened through the advertisement columns or in some other way (this will be checked on tomorrow). Probably what was suggested to Loëm was not a straight exchange or a purchase, but an exchange involving the payment of a certain sum on his part. (Sergeant Janvier, who is also something of a philatelist, tells me that there are some much dearer stamps, including the Mauritius penny vermilion, valued at between five hundred and six hundred thousand francs.) This would square with the sum which Loëm had on him when he went to keep the appointment. It also squares with Fred's mentality for he must have had the idea of demanding payment in dollars.

Lucas, who was feeling hot, created a draught by opening the door and the window of the adjoining office, that of the Chief of the Vice Squad.

It was at this meeting that the financier was killed in his own car. The murderer was almost certainly Fred, and it may be assumed that the Count, if he was present, disapproved of this method, because I know what a coward he is.

Did Lili keep watch? This is something to be established.

The fact remains that the murderers were interrupted by the Mouse's arrival, and that the tramp, by some means or other, came into possession of the wallet.

Lucas woke Janvier up.

'Go round to the corner of the Faubourg Montmartre, where there's a bar open all night, and bring back a bottle of brandy . . .'

He had to think of everything, in this report, to construct a whole theory on suppositions.

Inspector Lognon, of the Municipal Police, is better qualified than anyone else to give a detailed account of the Mouse's movements. It should be noted that, if it had not been for the initiative taken by this officer, no legal action would be possible.

And Lucas shrugged his shoulders as he thought of the unobtrusive silhouette of Madame Lognon, her rain-sodden hat, her grey cotton gloves.

The Mouse's ruse, now that we know the exact contents of the wallet, is easy to understand . . .
. . . Fred's long stay in America enabled him to carry out this business using methods which are fortunately not very common in France.
. . . only a careful investigation, or perhaps a stroke of luck, can tell us how he managed to get rid of both the body and the victim's car . . .

The report already covered five large pages, which he re-read carefully. Then he added:

Note: In spite of the discretion observed by all the gentlemen of the Basle Group, it seems clear that Müller, a minor employee, accidentally discovered his chief's liaison, and, by blackmailing him, obtained the position which he occupies today.
Falling in love with Mademoiselle Staori in the course of a visit to Budapest, he himself became the tool of an unscrupulous lawyer who tried, through him, to involve Loëm in a rather dubious enterprise.
In Budapest, the financier, having made inquiries, refused to meet the lawyer.
Müller cannot have been tough enough. In spite of everything, he retained a healthy respect for the power of the gentlemen of the Basle Group.
Hence the girl's annoyance, the attitude she adopted, her hysterical outburst and her threats.

'What a farce!' sighed Lucas as Janvier came back with a bottle of cheap brandy.

'What's a farce?'

'Having to do all this work for nothing . . .'

'Why for nothing?'

'You'll see!'

The future proved him to be right. Yet he did everything that had to be done. The following morning, after dozing for an hour on a sofa in the waiting-room, he ordered the four men to be brought into his office, and handed each of them a typewritten copy of his report. While they were reading, he did not even watch them: it was not worth it. Fred finished first and declared:

'Ten out of ten!'

'You've got nothing to add?'

'Me? Nothing at all!'

'And you?'

The Count turned his head away and muttered:

'Nothing.'

'Same here!' said Lili with a grin. 'If you think you're going to get a conviction with that, you can think again!'

The Mouse remained in his corner and just as he was about to go out behind the others, Lucas shut the door.

'Well?'

'Nothing . . .'

'Is there anything wrong in that report?'

The Mouse looked at the door through which his companions had disappeared. It was the most memorable moment in his life. With a lump in his throat, he said:

'It's all true!'

'Did you see them?'

'No.'

'They weren't in the car?'

'I don't know, I swear I don't! And this time you can

believe me! I really do swear it! What's going to happen to me?'

'Three months,' said Lucas laconically.

'Not more than that? you're sure?'

'Possibly with suspended execution of sentence . . . For attempted fraud and making a false statement to the police...'

'Ah well . . .'

And his shoulders dropped in resignation.

. . . supports the application of Inspector Lognon who would make a good inspector at Police Headquarters provided . . .

Lucas's pen remained in the air for a moment.

. . . that he resigns himself to curbing his enthusiasm and to seeking his superiors' approval before taking the initiative . . .

Judge Séverin spent a month on the case, the hottest month in the year, and the most unpleasant when a man's whole family is at Houlgate and he cannot even join them on Sundays.

'I don't know what it's all about,' Fred kept repeating confidently.

'You're beginning to get on my nerves with your Loëms and your Archibalds . . .'

Lili had been released on bail and was once again to be seen in the bars of the Place des Ternes.

. . . all three accused of abduction, violence, and impersonating police officers . . .

Because of the business of the Mouse and Fouquet's. As for the rest, there was nothing to be done. There was still no corpse and the gentlemen from Basle had left Paris, as had Müller, the latter for China, while Miss Dora had become engaged in Berlin to one of Hitler's young lieutenants.

The blow Lognon had received on his head had left him with a nervous twitch: his left eyelid went up and down spasmodically, so that he looked as if he were perpetually winking. As he had been put on duty watching the main-line stations, there were two incidents, because women travellers complained of his insolent attitude.

As for the Mouse, one dreary day towards the end of July, he went along to the Avenue du Parc-Montsouris. He was dragging his left leg with a certain weariness, for he had just completed four weeks of preventive detention, a circumstance which had led the court to treat him leniently.

'Madame Boisvin?' he asked the concierge of one apartment house.

'What do you want with her?'

'I'd like to see her . . .'

'Well, you'd have to go to Brittany to do that, because she's on holiday there with the little boy . . .'

The little boy who, to the joy of the gentlemen of the Basle Group, was not called Loëm but Boisvin, a fact which had led them to make a once-for-all payment of one hundred thousand francs by way of indemnity.

The best thing to do, they told her, was to open a little shop . . .

But Lucile Boisvin preferred to make hats at home for the young women of the district.

Three months for Fred, two months for Lili, and three months plus banishment from Paris (on account of his previous convictions) for the Count, who now cut a very sorry figure.

The summer went by. It was only on 21 September that a barge nearly sank. In order to unload a cargo of sand, she had left the main arm of the Seine downstream from the Île de Puteaux, and had entered the narrower arm which followed the Boulevard not far from the new blocks of flats. There, where the inland navigation charts guaranteed ten feet of water and anglers knew a hole fifteen feet deep which was splendid for chub-fishing, the boat had struck an obstacle which had made a hole in her side.

A diver was sent for. Nobody bothered about this incident, until a report reached Police Headquarters.

. . . have discovered a car with dented bodywork, and in this car the unrecognizable corpse of a man who . . .

There followed the number of the car Y.A.5–6713.

Loëm's car . . .

Lucas was on holiday at Biarritz, and his substitute questioned Fred for two hours, without being able to pin anything on him.

Immediately the gentlemen of the Basle Group, all twelve of them this time, arrived in Paris, one of them even coming from Istanbul. It was possible to draw up the death certificate. It was possible to open the will.

The newspapers said:

It seems, as far as can be judged in view of the condition of the corpse, that the Swiss financier skidded and that . . .

. . . his fortune, which amounts to about one hundred million Swiss francs . . .

And the Mouse, who was reading this in the poor light of the Opera station, pinched the nose of his neighbour, an old Czech, to stop his snoring.

One hundred million Swiss francs! Possibly a thousand, ten thousand, a hundred thousand presbyteries . . .

1938

More About Penguins

If you have enjoyed reading this book you may wish
to know that *Penguin Book News* appears every month.
It is an attractively illustrated magazine containing
a complete list of books published by Penguins and
still in print, together with details of the month's
new books. A specimen copy will be sent free on
request.

Penguin Book News is obtainable from most bookshops;
but you may prefer to become a regular subscriber at
3s. for twelve issues. Just write to Dept EP, Penguin
Books Ltd, Harmondsworth, Middlesex, enclosing
a cheque or postal order, and you will be put on the
mailing list.

Some other books published by Penguins are described
on the following pages.

Note: *Penguin Book News* is not available
in the U.S.A.

In Case of Emergency

Georges Simenon

Few writers pierce the plaster of normality and respectability with such a disturbing effect as Georges Simenon.

In Case of Emergency is the self-portrait of a French defence counsel whose gilt-edged success has been based on a series of dubious cases and who now moves in a world of politicians, ambassadors, business-men, and fashionable women. Maître Gobillot is suddenly impelled, nevertheless, to embark on a secret diary ... to open a dossier on himself. Yvette, the prostitute whose defence he had rigged, who brazenly offered to pay with her body, who afterwards became his mistress ... Yvette provides the impulse. But Gobillot knows his confession must go deeper than a recent obsession with a girl.

Simenon gives the reader a clear-cut impression of a ruthless but honest personality who is moving towards a crisis in which, with all his values in the melting-pot, tragedy switches off the heat.

The Widower

Georges Simenon

Unlike the majority of novelists, Georges Simenon is not content with a flat portraiture of people. Again and again he reveals his characters in depth and suggests with astounding insight how they have become what they are.

As a child Bernard Jeantet had been called clubfooted; patiently he had trained himself to mask his disability. Now a painstaking, meticulous free-lance designer, he has been married for eight years, but there are no children. His wife, Jeanne, was a prostitute: he had rescued her one night when her ponce slashed her with a knife in the street outside his flat. He supposed she was happy.

Suddenly Jeanne disappears without a word, and Bernard's narrow world of illusion is shattered. With the discovery of her ugly fate, we see a timid, impotent character rudely faced with the unattractive truths about himself. But can he profit by the successive revelations?

NOT FOR SALE IN THE U.S.A. OR CANADA

Black Rain

Georges Simenon

Henry Miller has remarked that Simenon would make a wonderfu, (benevolent) dictator, who would provide real bread and real winel and not the ideological varieties that give us mental and moral constipation.

Black Rain, the second of the two long stories in this volume, reconstructs with the reality and precision of Tolstoy a child's recollections of his home in a little town in Normandy. There is something akin to Simenon's great novel, *Pedigree*, in this faithful portrait of a family and the account of the ruthless hunt for an anarchist on the run.

The Survivors, however, with its exact account of the return of a trawler to Fécamp and the arrest of the popular skipper on a charge of murder, is a mystery story in the manner of the Maigret books.

Both these stories were written over twenty years ago. They provide many contrasts with the more curt and impressionistic manner of Simenon's later work.

NOT FOR SALE IN THE U.S.A.

SIMENON

André Gide François Mauriac, and other famous French writers have been among the admirers of Georges Simenon, who is not only one of the most talented novelists but also one of the most prolific. English critics, too, for many years have been lavish in their praises:

'Simenon seems to me a man of genius' – Raymond Mortimer in the *Sunday Times*

'One of the great writers of our time' – Ralph Partridge in the *New Statesman*

'The best living detective-writer . . . Maigret is the very bloodhound of heaven' – C. Day Lewis (Nicholas Blake) in a broadcast

The following books by Simenon are available in Penguins:

Fiction
Act of Passion   Black Rain*
In Case of Emergency   The Little Man from Archangel
The Man Who Watched the Trains Go By†   Pedigree*
The Premier   The Stain on the Snow†
Striptease   Sunday
The Widower

Crime
The Hatter's Ghosts   Inquest on Bouvet
Maigret Afraid   Maigret and the Burglar's Wife
Maigret in Court   Maigret at the Crossroads†
Maigret and the Enigmatic Lett†   Maigret's Failure
Maigret's First Case   Maigret and the Hundred Gibbets†
Maigret Meets a Milord†   Maigret and the Old Lady
Maigret and the Reluctant Witnesses   Maigret in Montmartre
Maigret's Mistake   Maigret Mystified†
Maigret's Revolver   Maigret in Society
Maigret Stonewalled†   Maigret has Scruples
Maigret Takes a Room   The Murderer*
My Friend Maigret

*NOT FOR SALE IN THE U.S.A.
REMAINDER NOT FOR SALE IN THE U.S.A. OR CANADA
†AVAILABLE IN THE U.S.A.